TAKEN

STAR BREED BOOK SEVEN

ELIN WYN

CLOCK
WALK
PUBLISHING

CINTHA

"You're not my mother!"

The door slammed hard enough to make the shelves rattle.

I flinched and prayed nothing would fall. Thankfully, nothing did.

This time.

With a sigh, I focused on carefully pouring the molten liquid into the mold, glad I hadn't dropped it when I'd flinched. The metal was stupid expensive and spilling even a drop would set me back.

Unfortunately, I had only a limited time to work with the metal before it cooled, which meant I couldn't go running after Talley, no matter how bad I wanted to.

But then, it was probably good to give her a bit of

space. She was at that age where, no matter what I did or said, it was the wrong thing.

Had I been like that when I was her age?

Yeah, probably.

But, to be honest, when I was her age I was busy sneaking out of an imperial orphanage, determined not to spend the rest of my life rotting there with the hundreds of other kids.

Back then, I'd thought I knew everything.

No doubt Talley thought the same thing.

Once I finished this piece and she'd had time to cool down, I'd go find her. We'd sit and talk and work it out, just like we always did.

The pendant seemed to take even longer than normal, though I know it didn't.

I'd done this work a thousand times now.

While the pendant would be beautiful once it was finished, it was no more ornate or time consuming than any of the others I'd made over the years since I'd set up shop here in the wild belly of Orem Station.

It was delicate work, which is why I couldn't let Talley help with it.

"I'm not a child!" she'd yelled at me, starting off this afternoon's rant.

If looks could kill, I'd have been dead right then and there.

I let out a huff as I laid the last gem in place.

Like I was keeping her away from this because of her age.

She'd been helping out in the shop for a couple years now and could do more than some jewelers I'd met. But still, working with therorium required patience and a steady hand, something she'd have one day.

One day.

Another year, maybe two, and I could start having her do simple pieces for me in the demanding stuff.

Until then, until her temper stopped flaring at the slightest discouragement, I'd have her stick to more forgiving materials.

Once I had everything safely locked back up, I flipped the closed sign on the door, then headed out to find where Talley had run off to.

I started with her normal hangouts, but no one had seen her today.

Of course not.

She couldn't make it easy for me to find her.

My shop was right at the fringe of the area known as the Under. It was one of the seedier places in the Empire, but it had been my home since escaping from the orphanage.

My best friend Loree had prided herself on working her way out of the Under, but I'd stayed here. Being here made it easier to keep an eye on Daix, my brother, and Talley, his daughter.

And, even if I hated to admit it, life outside seemed just a little boring.

Safe.

I ventured further and further into the depths of Under. It had a kind of unplanned beauty to it, something you couldn't replicate on purpose, no matter how hard you tried.

Though, as I stepped around a puddle of unidentifiable sludge, wrinkling my nose, the place could use a little bit more cleanliness.

Things had been straightening up on the station. The worst of the crime had been pushed further away since a group of mercenaries had made Orem Station their home base. Rumors flew about them.

Spies for the Emperor.

Pirates.

Inhuman.

But the ones I'd seen on patrol had been human-looking enough, even if they were big.

One even came into my shop pretty regularly, lips in a half-smile, golden eyes missing nothing.

There was a deep, dangerous attraction to him.

I'd hate to have him as an enemy, but he'd been nothing but quiet and kind to me.

And, he wasn't anywhere around right now, so all this daydreaming wasn't a bit of help.

Where in the Void had that girl gotten off to?

It'd been too long. I tried to stamp down the panic welling up inside me.

She was just being stubborn, trying to get a rise out of me.

Well, it's working, I thought with a frown.

A group of boys hung out on one of the street corners.

I recognized a few of them, one of the street gangs filled with kids and young teens. In the Upper and Lower, those gangs were mostly harmless. Just bored kids out getting into mischief.

Down here though, they were feeders for real trouble.

I'd done everything I could to keep Talley away. She hung around with some of them, though.

Most of the boys weren't bad people. They just didn't have many options in life and did what they needed to to survive.

Just like Daix.

And me.

And Loree.

We'd gotten lucky, though. Loree and I had found ways to survive that got us out of the streets, kept us from throwing our lives away.

If only Daix could've found something he was good at other than stealing, maybe we'd all be out of the Under right now.

"Hey, Zeek," I shouted to one of the boys I recognized.

He was the leader of the crew that controlled the territory around my shop. Though he had to be nearly seventeen now and would probably move into one of the adult gangs soon enough. He and I had an understanding.

My shop was off limits and in exchange, I always kept some extra food on hand for him and the others.

Even in the crews, most of them just barely scraped by, barely surviving. And I remembered all too well what it was like to go hungry at night.

"What's up, Cintha?" he shouted back, grinning at me.

His clothes were fairly new, still in good condition. If that hadn't been enough, the handle of a permasteel knife peeked out of his right boot, shouting his status.

The other boys looked at me warily when I walked up, but with a flick of his head, Zeek sent them away, off on some business I didn't want to think about too much.

"You seen Talley around?" I asked, keeping my voice low and even.

Just because we had an understanding didn't mean I wanted Zeek to hear the panic in my voice. Fear was a weakness in their eyes and he wouldn't hesitate to exploit that if he thought it would benefit him.

"Why? You and her have a fight again?" Zeek grinned at me, showing off perfectly white and straight teeth. A rarity in these parts, more credits, more status.

I shrugged, fighting to keep my face neutral. "You know how girls her age are. If it's not one thing, it's something else."

Zeek laughed and nodded. "Yeah, I get you. I saw her heading down toward the warehouses. She looked pissed about something."

I let out a sigh, shaking my head. This girl really was going to be the death of me one of these days.

"When you gonna let her join up with us, huh? You know we can use a girly with her talents." Zeek smirked while I just rolled my eyes.

It was a familiar conversation between us, one he knew damn well he was never going to win. He wanted a girl who knew jewelry, could tell them what stuff was worth. I didn't want her getting mixed up in any of that.

"At least with us you wouldn't have to worry about her. We'd keep her safe."

"Yeah, until the new guards come pay you guys a visit. You think they're gonna let her off easy just 'cause she didn't actually steal any of it?" I raised an eyebrow, meeting his gaze.

"We haven't been busted yet," he said with the easy cockiness of youth.

He'd survived everything life had thrown at him thus far, so he thought he was invincible.

Even for these boys, who'd lived by the skin of their teeth their entire lives, they still thought they knew it all, could handle anything.

Until something they couldn't handle came along.

"It'll happen one day," I warned him, but he just shrugged it off. I didn't have time to worry about him, though.

One stubborn kid was all I could handle.

"You stay safe, okay?"

"Always," he replied. The way his cheeks colored slightly told me he didn't often have people say such things.

But then, most of the boys out here didn't have anyone to care for them. It's why they'd joined the gangs, to watch out for each other. "You, too."

As I walked toward the warehouses, the fight with Talley looped over and over again in my ears.

No matter how much I tried to take care of her, I never would be her mother.

And it was the truth.

She'd never get to know her real mother, who'd overdosed when she was just a little one.

And I might love my brother, but he was a terrible father.

He'd been absent more than not her entire life.

And lately, he'd just been gone. Missing, not even a check-in.

No wonder she was in free fall.

One day she'd understand. I'd do anything to keep her safe, give her a talent, a future.

Assuming she didn't do something stupid before then.

Deeper into the docks I worked, stepping around crashed-out junkies, piles of scrap that no one wanted, and folks just looking for a place to sleep.

Then I froze.

"Come on, girlie, don't make this hard on us," a thickly accented voice said, not even trying to keep his voice down.

I searched wildly for the speaker, but he was out of sight. The tone made my heart run cold for some reason.

Part of me wanted to turn around, to head back down where I'd come from.

But Talley was out here somewhere.

And that wasn't an option.

Maybe I should've asked Zeek to come with me to find Talley. Even most of the adults down here wouldn't go through the effort of hassling me if I was with him and his crew.

But I'd come out here alone.

Zeek wasn't the only overconfident one, I kicked myself.

A shriek made me jump, my heart pounding faster and faster.

"Let me go!" a girl yelled.

Talley yelled.

Damn.

I cursed under my breath, really wishing I had a crew with me now.

Keeping as quiet as possible, I stepped up to the corner of a berth and peered around.

Talley was there, about halfway down, with four men blocking the only way out.

My heart beat even faster, the sound drumming in my ears, as I tried to figure some way to get her out of there.

A quick look around told me no one else was nearby, no one I could get help from.

I was on my own.

It wouldn't be the first time.

Their focus fixed on Talley, none of them noticed me slip up behind them until I kicked what I assumed to be leader straight between the legs. He dropped to his knees with a howl of pain as the other three spun to face me.

"Run," I shouted at Talley. "Go back toward the shop. Zeek's out there. He'll get you back there safely."

As much as Zeek wanted her as part of his crew, I knew he wouldn't let anything happen to her, even if she wasn't one of his.

He'd want a favor later, but I'd be willing to trade.

Trades and favors, that's what the Under ran on.

"But--" Talley whimpered.

"Go!" I yelled. "I'll be right behind you!"

Eyes wide, she sprinted past the men and away from the docks.

One of the guys tried to grab her, but I rammed into him, using all of my weight to make him stumble backwards a few steps.

It didn't knock him down, but it gave Talley enough time to disappear out of sight, at least.

The downside was tackling him put me right in the middle of them, just like Talley had been.

And no one was coming to help me.

Void.

I should've been thinking, should've been smarter.

Just because I wasn't a street kid anymore, just because I'd gotten myself set up with a shop, didn't mean I could stop looking over my shoulder.

One of the guys grabbed my arms and held me.

I struggled, trying to break his grip, but it was useless.

The one I'd kicked in the balls stepped up in front of me, grinning. "Well, it's not the girlie, but she'll have to do. Different market, but she'll still fetch a good price."

Breath tight in my chest, I tensed for a fight.

Then the man's fist flashed forward, and everything went black.

LORCAN

I tapped my fingers on the table, studying the man seated across from me. Big, as much muscle as fat, and supposed to be intimidating.

For most people, he probably did the trick.

Unfortunately for him, I was a long way from most people.

We'd been here for hours, going round and round in circles.

I didn't want Durl, I wanted his boss, the one running the show.

If I took out this lump, there'd just be another brainless muscle-head sitting in his place by this time next week.

Take out his boss, though... and we could bring down the entire racket.

Whoever Durl worked for had a big enough stake in trafficking humans that it'd put a serious dent into the market.

Which is why Ronan had sent me here to put up with Durl's thick-headedness rather than just beating the information out of him.

Of all of my brothers, I had the reputation for being cold.

Calculating.

It was a useful skill, even if it wasn't exactly accurate.

If his boss got even a tingling that someone was after him, he'd disappear like a puff of smoke in the wind. I wasn't going to risk that happening, not by a long shot.

So, I put up with Durl for now.

Until he handed me his boss on a silver platter, I'd keep putting up with him.

Even if tossing him across the bar was looking more and more tempting.

"Look," I finally said, leaning across the table, attempting to keep my voice level, even while I thought about how easy it'd be to pull out his trachea. "I need a considerable amount of labor. 'Bots ain't gonna cut it. They're too expensive to maintain. People, though? They're easy and cheap to replace. So, unless your boss wants me to take my business elsewhere, he'll stop hiding behind his lackey and come do business like a real man. I've already bought a handful from you, but if we're going to do real business, he's going to have to step up. It's how I've always run my operations and I don't see any reason to change."

Durl let out a huff and crossed his arms in front of his chest. The look on his face told me he was considering teaching me a lesson.

Please.

I briefly wondered how far I could push him. If he threw the first punch, if he cracked, it would give me the excuse I so desperately wanted to kick his ass without blowing my cover.

No such luck.

"You must have a death wish," the guy practically growled at me. "Don't know if you're brave or just damn stupid."

I just shrugged. There wasn't much reason to get into a battle of wits with a half-wit.

Either he'd relay my message to his boss and get me my meeting or I'd have to find another way to infiltrate their organization.

Annoying, but doable.

A waitress walked over, showing more skin than not. "Can I get you fellas anything?" She batted her eyelashes and wiggled a bit, leaving me no doubt about the definition of that 'anything'.

But a tame, perfunctory roll, even if it filled some of the time Durl was wasting, wasn't going to do anything to take the edge off my appetites.

Durl ordered a drink, but I waved her off.

I wanted my mind sharp and alert, just in case things ended up going south.

Doc had given me a lot of advantages. I wasn't enough of an idiot to slow those down.

After the waitress wandered off, Durl glared at me one more time, then started tapping away on a datpad.

I leaned back in my chair, scanning the bar. At least my message was being passed along up the chain.

On Outlander Terminal, you usually didn't want to get caught sticking your nose into someone else's business. It was a good way to end up dead.

I had no intention of ending up dead. Nor did I care about whatever petty crimes these folks were neckdeep in. All I cared about was Durl and his little trafficking ring.

While there were high-class joints on Outlander Terminal, this wasn't one of them.

The false windows were caked over with generations of grime, and the air was thick with smoke from synthhash, as well as some other, harder drugs.

It was a wonder anyone could breathe while they were in here. Then again, most of them were probably too drugged or drunk to notice the heavy air.

While Orem had been making strides becoming a bit more legitimate under Granny Z's reinforced rule, Outlander Terminal made no such promises and never would.

Then a woman walked by the table, catching my eye. For a second, I thought it was Cintha, a jeweler back on Orem.

It was possible I'd volunteered for a few extra shifts helping Granny Z's forces patrol the Under.

And maybe I'd stopping in her shop, just to make sure things were alright. She worked hard, and was a friend of Xander's mate Loree.

Besides, now that so many of my brothers had mates, there would probably need to be presents, and baby things, and...

Really.

It had nothing to do with the halo of her hair, or her quick smile when she crafted a piece just right.

How her deft fingers spun metal into beauty.

The woman across the room turned.

My chest loosened and I sank back into my chair.

Of course, it wasn't her.

Cintha would have no reason to be on Outlander.

Good thing, because, for a moment, I'd been ready to march her out of this dive and send her curvy ass back to Orem, where she'd be safe.

Durl's datapad chirped, and I refocused. But before

Durl could even look at the message, a commotion broke out. The man at the table next to us stood up roughly, the chair skittering backwards before toppling over. He slammed his fists down on their table, shouting at the guy he'd been sitting with.

Idiots.

They were both drunk or drugged or maybe both, slurring as they traded insults. Whatever was going on, it didn't concern me, and I had no intention of getting involved.

I turned my attention back to Durl, fixing him with my gaze. When I cleared my throat, he looked back over at me, clearly annoyed at me interrupting the show.

Void forbid this man do some actual work.

It was going to be a small miracle if we got through this meeting without me losing my fabled control.

When the one man lunged across the table at the other, I let out a low growl. The two men wrestled on the floor until they crashed into my chair, which was more than enough to set me over the edge.

I glared at the two men as I stood, grabbing them both by the back of the neck and easily lifting them into the air.

As I marched toward the door, the crowd parted in front of us. These guys may have been some of the biggest outlaws in the Empire, but even they weren't stupid enough to get in the way.

At the entrance, I kicked open the door, then tossed both men onto the corridor. They landed with a rough tumble, groaning as they did so.

Then I turned back to the rest of the bar, glaring at them all, daring them to do or say something. "If anyone else wants to act like children, take it outside," I said before walking back to where I'd been sitting. I placed both hands on the table and glared down at Durl, my patience more than worn through.

"Well?"

Durl sat still, his hands balled into fists, his knuckles white. It looked like he was ready to shit himself. Either that or run out the door after the two I'd just tossed out.

"Are we doing business or should I go elsewhere?" I prompted.

Durl finally seemed to remember what he was there for.

He nodded, then stood. "You've got your meeting. Though you may regret it. We'll contact you with the time and place."

"Good," I said, then turned my back on him and walked out. I kept my senses alert, just in case he decided to try and brain me from behind, but by the time I crossed the threshold of the bar, he still hadn't moved from the table.

CINTHA

My head pounded, my mouth dry.

I rubbed my eyes, hissing at the dull pain there. Then it all came flooding back to me. With a groan, I leaned back against the hard, cold wall.

I'd been so stupid, going after those guys without any help, without any plan.

And I'd do it again to get Talley out of there.

I opened my eyes and looked around, my worst fears having come to life. I wasn't still in that berth, just nursing a headache after getting into a fight I couldn't lose.

Nope, I was locked in some dingy little cell with at least a dozen other people.

And the deck hummed under my hands.

Not the regular rhythm of Orem as it spun in space, the subconscious heartbeat we all lived and worked to.

This was different.

This was a ship.

Heading to Void knows where. Once again, I cursed myself for being such a foolish idiot. How in the world was I going to get myself out of this one?

Well, at least I wasn't shackled. That would definitely make things a bit easier. Maybe once we landed there'd be a chance to slip off somewhere, find someone who could help me.

It'd been a long time since I'd had to smuggle myself aboard a transport ship, but I had a feeling I could still do it. Especially since I had a pretty damn good motivation.

Looking around the cell, though, my heart ached.

Most of them were just children, all around Talley's age or a bit older, with a couple other women my age. None of them looked to be in the best shape, all gaunt and dirty. Street people, no doubt.

No, if I was going to get out of here, I was going to make sure to take all of them with me.

I scooted over to where one of the women was sitting, her legs drawn up against her chest. Even in the low light, I could make out bruises up and down her arms and legs. I clenched my fists, wanting to hurt whoever had done that to her.

Good, sensible, safe Cintha needed to be gone for a bit.

Fighting, surviving Cintha was back.

"Hey," I said, keeping my voice low. "Do you have any idea where we are?"

A flood of questions ran from my tongue. Who took us? Where were we heading? Why? All of that would have to factor into any plans I had to get us out of here and back home.

But the woman shook her head. There were tears at the corner of her eyes, but she refused to let them fall.

A young woman who'd been through hard times before, was trying her hardest to convince herself she could get through this, too.

I knew that feeling very well.

"Where are you from?" I asked her, hoping that would be a better topic, one I could work some other answers from.

She blinked, trying to dispel the tears. When she spoke, her voice was soft and hoarse. "A town called Cynna on Ryak IV."

I bit my lower lip to hold back curses. Ryak IV was a good ways away from Orem. So, these guys weren't just taking people from Orem. They were grabbing people from wherever they could.

"Are there others here from Ryak IV?"

The woman nodded and pointed to two others, a

girl around Talley's age and a boy a bit older, just on the cusp of manhood.

But no one else.

So, they were being smart, only taking a couple people from each place. Which meant they had a lower chance of getting caught.

Kidnapping and trafficking people was one of the few things the pirate ruler of Orem had no tolerance for.

Probably the same in the rest of the Empire, but I wouldn't know.

The woman, Nika, slowly came out of her shell, introducing me to the others who had been there longer.

They'd been taken from a grand total of four places, including Orem. All were people who wouldn't be missed when they disappeared, people they could easily get alone and slip off with.

None of them had families or friends who would look for them.

Except me. Talley would be looking for me. Maybe even Daix, whenever he turned up again. Loree, the next time she remembered to come down and check on things.

It wouldn't take long for my clients to notice I was gone, either.

Maybe, just maybe, the mercenary with the golden eyes.

And... that was it.

Well, maybe it wasn't much of a social life, but with any luck, that mistake would cost them, one tiny chip in their plan that would unravel the entire thing.

Someone would come looking for me, eventually.

I wouldn't bet on it, though, not with the lives of myself and everyone else who'd been taken. I had to take care of myself and those who needed me, just like I'd always done.

I surveyed the room, but couldn't see any way out. The walls and door looked to be made of permasteel, with just a small slit in the door for someone to look in on us.

Definitely not something we could easily get out of.

Even if we did manage to get out of here, if we were in space, there wasn't anywhere else for us to go.

I'd picked up a number of skills on the streets, but piloting a starship?

A bit out of my league.

I'd have to bide my time, keep an eye on things, and see what options presented themselves. When they landed again, we could get out and make a break for it, find someone who could help us, protect us.

There were few places that wouldn't lend aid to a

group of women and children kidnapped by traffickers, if we could get off the ship.

A commotion outside the room made everyone back up against the wall, retreating into themselves. Whatever or whoever was coming clearly terrified them all. Which could work in my favor.

If I played my cards right, waited until the right time, it might be possible to overpower even a handful of guards. These people were malnourished and weakened, but I'd learned never to bet against someone's survival instincts.

When the door slammed inward, everyone jumped, including me. A big, squint-eyed man walked inside, tall, easily a head taller than me. He had big, bulging muscles, the kind the enforcers for the gangs usually had. He was bald, but with a bushy beard like he was trying to make up for it.

His clothes were old and worn, but clean, not a speck of dirt. Just like with the gangs back on Orem, the clothes told you a lot about a person. And his clothes told me he was near the top of the food chain. Not at the top, no, not a man like him, but he definitely wasn't out doing the grunt work anymore.

He wouldn't be an easy one to take down, even with all of us against him. Not impossible, though. I'd learned long ago that even men like that had a weakness, particularly between their legs.

The man surveyed the room, eying each person. He had a scowl on his face as he looked at all of us. "Pathetic waste of space, if you ask me. Can't see why anyone'd be willing to pay for any of you. Never should've taken this damn job."

Despite his words, he came into the cell, walking over to each person and looking them up and down. It was a look I'd seen often on men like him, the lecherous bastard. Even the boys and girls weren't spared his roving eyes, not that I was all that surprised. A man like him wasn't usually particular in who he used to satisfy himself.

"Aren't you a pretty thing?" he said, stopping in front of Nika.

Void, she was barely into adulthood.

When the man squatted down in front of her to get a better look, she scurried backward, drawing her knees up to her chest and wrapping her arms around them. She was absolutely terrified.

But of course she was.

She'd been a street kid not long ago, if I guessed right. She knew exactly what a man like this would want.

Damn if I was going to let him have it, though.

I stood and moved away from where I'd been sitting. "Leave her alone," I said, balling my hands into fists and gritting my teeth.

There wasn't a whole lot I'd be able to do against him on my own, but if he thought he was just going to have his way with whoever he wanted, then he was going to have to go through me to do it.

He looked over at me, then frowned and stood. "You got a problem?" He sneered at me. "You jealous? You want a little attention for yourself? You got a bit more meat on your bones. I bet you're used to taking care of men to get by. So, what about it, you want to make things a little more comfortable for yourself?"

I glared at him as he walked over to me. "Not a chance," I told him, keeping my voice even.

The man's face hardened as his scowl returned. He took a few long strides, until he stood right in front of me. "You sure got a mouth on you. Bet I can think of a better use for it."

"Only if you want me to bite it off," I challenged. "Think I won't?"

The man got right up into my face. He was seething now, I could see it in the way the veins on his forehead and neck bulged. Maybe if I kept it up he'd have an aneurysm and drop dead at our feet. Wouldn't that be a turn of luck?

The chances of that happening, though, were pretty damn slim, even as he seemed to get angrier and angrier. I should've been scared of him, should have been terrified, just like everyone else in the cell. But I refused to cower from a man like him, refused to let him have the satisfaction of scaring me.

Instead, I focused on distracting myself by focusing on the smaller details, like his mottled skin or the numerous red veins running through the white parts of his eyes. This close, I could practically count the hairs in his beard if I'd wanted to. My reaction seemed to be working, though, and he got madder and madder. While he let out a stream of curses and threats, I just focused on memorizing every last detail I could.

The man shoved me backward. I stumbled under his strength, my head smacking into the permasteel wall, stars spinning in front of my eyes. But before I had a chance to clear my head, the man's hand flew forward as he backhanded me. At first, there was just a loud crack as his hand hit my skin. Then, almost as if on a delay, the shooting pain came.

Fuck, it hurt, but at least I hadn't blacked out this time. I did slump down the wall, though, as my breath came in ragged gasps. I glared up at the man, refusing to let him see me cry, not matter how much the right side of my face hurt. I had no doubt there'd be a bruise there, probably one to match the black eye I'd gotten protecting Talley.

"Worthless piece of trash," the man spat as he snarled down at me. "I should brain those idiots for bringing you aboard. You're not worth the credits we'll get for you."

He turned and glared at everyone else in the cell. Then, his eyes locked on Nika again and my breath hitched. Would he still go for her? But then he spat on the deck before stomping out of the cell, slamming the door shut behind him.

Nika and another woman rushed over to me, checking that I was okay. "You're either very brave or very, very stupid," Nika told me, her lips curved up into the barest smile.

I grinned back at her. "A little of both, I'd wager."

LORCAN

The whine of the shuttle filled my ears. Sitting in the back, without so much as a window or a view screen, was starting to get on my nerves.

All I could do was sit there, eyes closed, and focus on my breathing.

There were worse places to be.

It was all another scare tactic.

The sense of the unknown was meant to unnerve me, but all it did was bore me. They wanted me to know I was out here alone, without even knowing where I was.

It was supposed to make me think twice about double-crossing them, knowing there wouldn't be any help out here.

What they didn't know was, I didn't need help.

Besides, being out in the middle of nowhere meant less of a chance of innocent casualties if it came down to a fight. Without anyone else around, I wouldn't have to hold back, wouldn't have to control myself.

I could let loose.

And that solitary thought was what kept me sane, stuck in that damn shuttle.

When we finally touched down, I couldn't help but grin. We were there. Finally, I was making progress.

The door finally slid open, Durl's ugly mug glaring at me. "Let's go," was all he said before turning and stalking away, clearly expecting me to follow him.

I considered just snapping his neck while his back was turned, then immediately discarded the idea.

As much as he annoyed me, it would be a risk I didn't need to take just yet. Besides, he may be a brain-dead oaf, but there was still information I could get out of him.

I hopped out of the shuttle, quickly surveying my surroundings.

There was a cluster of buildings all connected to one another, all protected by a large dome surrounding the area. If I had to guess, judging by the dry, lifeless rock beneath our feet, I'd say we were on a large asteroid. Which made sense. Criminal empires liked asteroids, since they were unclaimed territory. They could easily set up shop without anyone being any the wiser. It wasn't like the Empire could inspect every floating rock.

But something else was interesting.

Under the dome keeping in all that tasty oxygen, there was gravity. Artificial, of course. No asteroid I knew of had enough mass to pull properly.

That meant someone had been clever enough to rig the rock, spin it like a ship, maybe boost with an artificial grav unit somewhere.

Someone clever would be worth meeting.

Durl didn't bother waiting to see if I was following him, just stomped from the shuttle's landing pad toward the nearest entrance, never looking back once.

He still seemed to be harboring a grudge over our last meeting, which just made me smirk. He was easy to rattle, easy to get under his skin.

That was good. With any luck, his boss would be the same way.

Even once we were inside the building, he marched down the corridors, perhaps trying to lose me. He'd have to try a lot harder than that, though.

I could follow him blindfolded, just from the sound of his boots clomping down the halls. I made note of each hallway and doorway as we walked, mentally mapping the place as we went. There was always a chance I'd need a quick exit and I didn't want to be stumbling around this place.

Durl finally stopped in front of a large permasteel door. He grunted and nodded toward it. "This is your room. Someone'll come get you when the boss is ready to see you."

Once I was inside, the door closed. I could hear Durl stomping back down the hall, though I didn't hear anything or anyone else.

The room wasn't massive. It had enough room for a bed, a desk, and some chairs that probably weren't nearly as comfortable as they appeared.

A poorly hidden security camera in the corner with a view of the bed and the desk.

No terminal.

Interesting again.

Not that surprising. I wouldn't give a stranger easy access to my systems, no one would.

I flicked the button of my shirt. And they didn't even know what, or who, Eris would insist, I was carrying.

But interesting that the prepared "guest" room had no access to anything, no way for a friendly businessman to even call home.

When the door slid open again. I was on my feet in an instant, bracing for an attack. But none came.

Instead, a woman stepped inside. She eyed me up and down, wrinkling her nose slightly. "Mr. Jann will see you now," she said, voice flat.

I followed her out of the room, still making note of all the corridors as we walked. "So, where exactly are we?" I asked, doing my best to sound conversational.

"Exactly where you wanted to be," she said. She kept her head straight forward, arms down by her sides, never glancing my way.

She didn't seem to mind talking - but her answers weren't anything useful.

It'd be easy to write her off as another lackey, but her words didn't have the ring of ignorance. They slid around my questions like a school of fish, flashing in the light, but impossible to pin down.

I kept a close eye on her, studying her body language. No way she was a serving girl, she was someone of some importance.

Someone I needed to watch.

She wouldn't be the first female crime boss we'd run into over the years.

For a racket of this size, a woman at the head wouldn't surprise me. People tended to be more trusting of women, which made it a lot easier for them to hide in plain sight.

She came to a stop right in front of another permasteel door, identical to the rest of them.

Few people would be able to easily navigate around this place, at least not without a lot of practice. Not everyone had my memory.

Instead of just walking in, though, she pressed a button next to the door and waited.

And for the first time I got a read of an emotion other than boredom from her.

Just a whiff of tension. Maybe irritation.

But whoever, whatever was in that room, she wasn't happy.

After a few moments, the door opened, and she walked in, me only a step behind her.

A man sat at a table in the center of the room. He stood when we walked in, grinning broadly, his arms spread wide.

"Mister Rand," he said with a pleasant tone. "Good to finally meet you. Welcome to the Dakar Belt."

The woman stepped aside as he walked over to us, hand outstretched. I took it, giving him a firm handshake, meeting him in the eyes.

Excited. Soft.

Definitely not the kind of man I'd expected to be running the largest human trafficking ring this side of the Empire.

And for all the woman's slipperiness about revealing the location of their operation, he'd let it out immediately.

Interesting again.

"It's a pleasure to finally meet you as well, Mister Jann."

"Oh, please, call me Brayden. Welcome to the Dakar Belt."

"Call me Logan, then," I replied, giving him the alias I'd chosen for this job. "I'm glad we can finally get down to business. I'm sorry if I was a bit rude with your man."

Brayden shrugged, looking every bit like he wouldn't have cared if I had snapped Durl's neck. "Pay him no mind. Durl has his uses, dealing with the small fires that come up. I much prefer to handle men like you myself."

I couldn't quite tell if that was a threat or not.

He said it with a smile, but then, how many men had I killed while pretending to be their best friend?

"It's easier to do business of this magnitude with the man in charge, rather than through a middle man." I smiled at him, laying on the charm. "I assume he did relay the details to you?"

Brayden nodded, then motioned to a seat at the table. As I sat, I raised an eyebrow towards the woman sitting at the edge of the desk.

Still irritated, just as silent.

Brayden waved in her general direction. "This is my sister, Teldra. She helps run some aspects of the business. Can't do everything myself, you know?"

I nodded. That explained why she knew so much about the operation and why he trusted her.

But not her attitude.

"As you know, since the re-emergence of the Empire into the Fringe quadrants, the rising costs of raw materials for machinery have started eating into profits of everyone's businesses. Machines break easily, need constant repair and maintenance. They're slowly becoming less and less useful for certain jobs." He leaned forward, steepling his fingers, his voice sliding into the patter of a well-rehearsed speech. "Which is where we come in. Human labor is once again becoming more and more a viable option."

It was all song and dance now.

He droned on, I made interested noises. Not too eager, just enough to keep the conversation going.

Smile at his jokes.

Allude to the large workforce I needed.

Scan the room for a terminal.

"I think we can accommodate you." Brayden glanced over at his sister. "We have enough to fulfill his demands, correct?"

Teldra nodded. "With the fresh arrivals, we do," she confirmed. Again, right to the point, very little emotion other than that slight undercurrent of oddness.

Maybe it had nothing to do with me, nothing to do with Brayden.

Maybe there was something in the business that had irritated her.

Void, if she had to deal with Durl on a regular basis, that would be enough.

As they talked back and forth, occasionally asking me a question, I started to zone out, to scan the room for any information I might need to file away. But the room was pretty bland, without much of anything identifiable.

Once, I thought I caught a whiff of Cintha's scent, then cursed myself.

Thinking about her in the middle of a job was stupid and foolish and reckless.

Thinking about her at all wasn't useful, either.

But Brayden droned on.

You'd think we were discussing a deal for any kind of goods, not human lives. He talked about the quality of the workers, their speed, how many years they had before they'd need to be replaced. He even had ones with specialties, should I need more than just menial labor.

The polite smiles and carefree attitude just made everything worse.

After this, I'd talk to Ronan and Davien about a nice, clean mission.

A bell chimed, making Brayden pause mid-sentence. He pressed a flat button set into the desk, then the door slid open.

So there was some sort of terminal access here. Useful.

A pretty blonde walked into the room, carrying a tray of drinks. She wore a tight, short dress that showed miles of leg, and didn't look comfortable in the least. If she bent over, we'd all probably be able to see right up it.

She set the tray on the table, then smiled at me.

Her eyes were oddly blank, a tiny scar at her temple.

Brayden put an arm around her, and she didn't flinch.

Just seemed...absent.

"You've had a long journey here. Perhaps you and Krissa here would like to go back to your quarters for a bit of.... rest?"

I fought down the bile that rose up in my throat.

I had no doubt she'd been kidnapped from somewhere, forced, and probably brainwashed into doing this for whatever men Brayden met with here.

I could take her, fight my way off the asteroid, take the shuttle.

And condemn every other man, woman, and child Brayden's operation touched.

This was why I was picked for the mission.

Cold.

Calculating.

I smiled and shook my head. "I'll pass for now."

Making a show of running my eyes up and down her body, I leaned back in the chair. "Perhaps later, though."

"Well then," Brayden said with a grin of his own. "Why don't we give you a tour of the facilities here? I'm sure you'll find it very interesting."

I nodded, glad he hadn't pushed it.

As we turned to the door, Teldra followed, eyes narrowed.

Something told me she noticed a lot more than she let on, was smarter than Brayden gave her credit for.

I would have to watch my back around her.

CINTHA

When the rumble of the ship's engines finally stopped with a jolt, my heart started pounding in my chest. I tried to stay calm, not wanting the others to see me panic.

If I was going to get us all out of here, I needed them calm, not making rash decisions.

And more than that, *I* needed to be calm and keep myself from making any rash decisions.

Everyone sat up when the sound of boots echoed closer and closer. But when the door opened this time, it wasn't the same guard from before. Two others, younger, but looking just as mean.

When they commanded us to follow, everyone walked with them without comment. They each carried heavy-looking batons that I knew would hurt.

This wasn't the time to make a break for it.

I kept my head straight forward as they led us off the ship and out of the docking area, but my eyes were constantly moving, taking in the surroundings.

Every piece of information mattered at this point, and you didn't grow up on the streets without learning to map an area out in your head.

We'd docked in an enclosed bay, stacks of cargo waiting for transfer out lining the walls.

But there wasn't the usual rush of crews from ship to ship, orders shouted, tools clattering to the deck.

Just an eerie silence.

No clues as to what sort of station we'd been brought to, where in the Empire or the Fringe we were.

Nothing but blank gray.

Finally, at yet another empty hallway, the guards separated us, sending a few into one room, a few into another, and then the rest of us into a third room.

My mouth filled with the taste of copper as I bit my tongue.

I wanted to fight back, to stop them from separating us, but I knew it would be futile. It wasn't like I could take the guards, and even if I could, where would we go?

We'd need to find help here, somehow. Surrounded by our enemies.

I blinked away tears as I shuffled into the third room, refusing to let them fall. I'd get out of here, get everyone out of here, eventually. One way or another, we'd all get away from whatever hellhole they'd dragged us to.

The man stopped in front of a large double door. Just the sight of it made a lump form in my throat.

It was permasteel and it looked like just one of the doors weighed twice as much as I did.

From inside, I could hear the whirring and clunking of machines.

He didn't say anything, just banged three times on the door, then stepped aside. Seconds after he was out of the way, it swung open and he shepherded us inside.

Beyond the doors was what looked like a large factory room, filled with people and machines, the noise growing even louder.

We were taken over to a far corner where another man waited, grinning like he'd just won the lottery. He was tall, though not quite as tall as the man who'd brought us here, and much thinner.

His hair was a greasy black and looked like it needed a good washing. "Thank you, Durl! I can take it from here."

The big, burly man grunted, then turned and left us. I glanced over my shoulder and watched as he walked back through the doors, then they swung shut behind him automatically. I couldn't make out any trigger that would've opened or closed the doors.

I frowned, wondering how they opened, then turned my attention back to the man in front of us.

"Well, then, now that you're here, let's get to work." The man's voice was friendly enough, but I didn't delude myself into thinking he cared about any of us. He may not have been as big as the other men I'd seen so far, but there was no doubt in my mind he was just as cruel. He wouldn't have been keeping us here, otherwise.

I watched as he showed each group of us how to assemble parts.

The work wasn't difficult, but I couldn't for the life of me figure out why they wanted us doing it. Surely robots could do this faster and more efficiently.

Why have a bunch of people doing it, instead? It didn't make any sense.

He grinned, and something deep in my gut shivered. "There's more than one kind of work here. If you do well, you have the opportunity to be promoted to the testing floor."

That sounded interesting. Maybe there'd be more chances there to figure out what was going on, where we were.

Still, I frowned, and watched everything the man showed us, committing it to memory. I wasn't sure how long I'd be stuck here, and I'd already made waves on the transport.

Getting killed or beaten unconscious on a regular basis wasn't going to help me get the hell out of here.

Over and over, we assembled and disassembled the same part until it seemed like I could do it blindfolded and in my sleep.

Then we moved on to the assembly line. The guy teaching us walked along the line behind us as we worked, keeping an eye on us. It was a bit unnerving, working with him constantly over my shoulder, but no worse than working with molten hot metals with a young girl underfoot.

"Remember, everyone!" the manager called out, "Perfect records mean promotions!"

Promotions.

Like this was a job that people had applied for.

But I noticed that the workers who'd been the in room before we arrived perked up. A promotion, whatever that meant, was something they wanted.

And if it was a good thing, then I wanted it, too.

At first, it was easy enough to assemble the parts. If anything, it was even easier than the jewelry work.

But then the conveyor belt bringing us the parts

picked up the pace. I had to focus to keep up and after a little while more, it went even faster.

I tried to help Nika, who was starting to lag behind. But the longer this went on, the harder it was for me to do my own pieces, let alone help with hers.

Both of us needed a break, but there didn't seem to be any kind of end in sight.

Hours passed until my hands ached and sweat dripped down my brow. My mouth was dry, my throat scratchy. I wasn't sure how much longer I could keep this up. My vision started to blur as I fought to stay focused on the parts.

That's when I noticed some of the parts weren't quite right.

At first, it was only a couple, spaced out here and there. Then it became more frequent. I frowned, trying to fix the pieces and get them down.

Now it was nearly impossible to keep up with the speed the parts were coming down the line. I was falling further behind and Nika was overwhelmed.

There wasn't a choice.

When the manager walked back, I waved him over.

He frowned as he approached. "Yes?" he asked, probably expecting me to complain about the speed things were coming.

Which I wanted to do, but guessed it would just fall

on deaf ears. Employee happiness didn't seem to be a priority with kidnappers and slavers.

"Some of these parts aren't assembled properly," I told him, holding one up to show him.

The man took the part from me and looked it over, his frown deepening. Then, he pushed past me to stand where I'd been, looking over all the parts that were now building up in my spot. More than two-thirds of them were assembled improperly now, with more arriving each second.

The man let out a rough sigh, then turned away without a word and stalked up the assembly line.

I stepped back into place, getting back to work, but keeping an eye on him. He headed over to two guards stationed against one wall. He said something to them, then they followed him back toward the lines.

The lines slowed down as he approached a man further up the line from me. Now I could watch them more easily, my hands working almost on autopilot by this time.

The guy who'd been teaching us pushed an older man aside, then picked up some of the parts and examined each of them. Then he tossed the parts back down onto the belt and turned toward the guards.

After a nod from him, the guards stepped forward. They grabbed the man on either side and lifted him off the ground. The man's legs kicked wildly as he shouted, babbling almost incoherently.

"No! I was promised to be a tester!"

I stared with my mouth wide open as they carried him from the room, still kicking and screaming like a child throwing a tantrum.

What kind of fate had I just condemned that man to?

LORCAN

I had to fight to keep from rolling my eyes as Brayden showed me around his facility. He was like a child showing off his prized toy.

Which would be fine if he was ten.

Also, if that toy wasn't ruining the lives of hundreds, if not thousands, of people across the Empire.

Near the beginning of the tour, Teldra split off from us. She'd barely said a word, though, so she wasn't missed very much, the absence of her radiating tension a minor relief.

When Durl and a guard named Horg joined up with us, I did miss her, just a bit. At least she wasn't loud and crass. They showed their disdain for the captives openly. It was obvious they thought nothing of these people, like they were less than even animals.

The longer we walked, the harder it was to keep my composure. Durl and Horg insisted on making comments and jokes as we surveyed each of the work groups on the assembly lines. They'd make comments about the women in particular, making me grit my teeth.

Control.

Calculate.

No matter what an individual suffered, the job was to rescue them all.

"As you can see, it's all very efficient," Brayden rambled on, looking every bit the proud father. Clearly, he was happy with the business he'd built himself. "If you have the right motivation, the right…. incentives… you'd be surprised just how well they can work."

Each of the rooms had a heavy guard presence, all of them looking rough, similar builds and expressions to Durl and Horg.

I could kill them. And Brayden. Everyone on this rock.

But until we had access to the files, until Nixie had access, really, it would just leave a power vacuum.

Calculate.

Brayden wasn't the only scum out there. Every one he'd dealt with, every one who'd supplied his victims, everyone who'd purchased 'merchandise' from him, every captain who'd hauled the cargo... We'd take out every last one of them.

Control.

Brayden patted me on the back, and I balled my hands into quick fists, letting my claws puncture into the flesh of my palms, the pain helping to clear my head a bit.

"Ready to go on and check out the next one?"

I smiled, mask firmly in place. "Absolutely. I'm very impressed with the operation thus far. I can see why you're so proud of it."

As we walked down another long corridor, Durl and Horg trailed behind us. Obviously there to take care of me if something got out of hand.

Amusing.

They were big, but not trained. Not paying attention to me, more interested in gossiping and making crude jokes.

"You should've seen the group I just brought in," Horg said to Durl with a laugh. "Only good for one thing, if you ask me. Was pretty damn tempting to sample the wares a bit on the way here! Fiesty little thing. May need to pay her a visit, after all."

Durl grunted, his voice echoing down the corridor. "You should have enjoyed them a bit! Given them a good time before they started working."

Brayden didn't look the least bit fazed. "Every job has its benefits, you know?"

I bit back the remark that threatened to leave my lips, then nodded and forced a smile, instead. "Of course they do. How else will you ensure quality employees that you trust?"

"Exactly!" Brayden beamed at me.

Nothing made sense. Here was a complicated, far-reaching operation.

But the man running it seemed to have the logical skills of an imbecile.

Was he playing me as much as I was playing him?

A high balcony circled each room, giving us a vantage point over the factory floor below.

Each process was different, but the workers looked the same. Exhausted-looking men and women fitting together random pieces of plex in meaningless patterns, over and over, any hope or spark in their eyes long gone.

A faint scent caught my attention.

"That's a lot of plex to be regenerating," I commented, wondering what the purpose was.

Brayden's eyebrows rose. "You're the first to notice! It's an important part of the training."

We walked to another room, his hands waving in his excitement to explain. "We're pre-training the workers for specific tasks and needs. We think of it as a wholesale operation. Obviously, some will be more suited to the assembly environment than others."

As we watched over the next room, he continued. "We weed out the workers that simply won't make it before delivery. And while fear is a motivator, we have other options."

Each finished piece of plex was tossed into a giant funnel. In a real factory, it'd be moved to the next assembly point, attached or further modified into something useful.

Here it was just melted back down, the acrid stench almost covering the scent of sweat and fear from the people below.

Another room. Another set of people, hands blindly working.

"By the time they leave us, they're well-trained for the exact operation our clients request. So we don't waste fuel on transporting defective workers, and they arrive ready to go."

I surveyed the room below.

There was something else there, a scent that tickled my senses, had every nerve on fire.

But between the general stench of fear and the continuous melting and remelting of the plex, I couldn't place it.

"It must have taken some capital to get the operation up and running this way," I acknowledged while I searched the floor. "It's a brilliant angle."

It was.

Sick, and heartless in its disregard for human life. Colder than even I could be in the reduction of people to replaceable cogs in a series of giant machines.

But brilliant.

Brayden bounced a little on his toes. "Teldra always says it's good for the two important things: a healthy bottom line and happy clients."

The wording slipped by me as I found what I sought.

It couldn't be.

Standing almost directly below the balcony was the last person I would have ever expected to see here.

The last person I would have ever *wanted* to see here.

Cintha.

My hands tightened around the railing as I stared down at her. My jaw set tight, a thousand things swarming through my head right that moment.

A strong part of me wanted to grab Brayden, throw him over the balcony, then jump down there, grab Cintha, and get the hell off this Void-forsaken rock.

Instead, I forced those feelings down deep inside me and turned to Brayden with a grin on my face.

"You know, I think I might take you up on that offer from before. Test out the goods?"

CINTHA

Sweat dripped down my forehead as I struggled to keep up with the pace of the conveyor belt. Now that the parts were all coming through properly assembled, it was slightly easier again, but it was still hard to keep up with my parts.

Plus, helping Nika with some of her work was really taking a toll on me.

But I wasn't going to see her dragged off the line like that other guy had been. No way was I going to risk that happening to either of us, which is the only reason I was able to keep going for as long as I had been.

We'd had one quick break for a meal, tasteless nutribricks still in the wrappers, but now we were back at it. I'd hoped for some information from the people who'd been here longer, suspicions as to where we were, what we were doing over and over.

But no one said anything. Either they were as confused as we were, broken into submission, or waiting, hoping their work would see them through to this mysterious promotion.

Back on the line, our trainer kept walking along behind us, keeping a close eye on things, making sure no one was falling behind or causing issues with the parts.

I kept my eyes on him, not wanting him to catch me helping Nika with her parts. Something told me he wouldn't be too appreciative of it, despite the work getting done.

A console on the far wall beeped, the loud, piercing sound echoing through the room. I risked a glance around and saw all the guards now standing at attention, their eyes glued to the panel.

The trainer rushed over to it, pressing a few buttons.

I could see him talking to it, but I couldn't hear anything he said or what was said back to him. The tension ramped up through the room, workers darting glances his way.

My stomach tightened. Whatever was happening couldn't be good.

When the trainer walked over to me, I thought I was

going to pass out. The look on his face told me something was going on, but my mouth was so dry I couldn't even ask. When he told me to follow him, I just nodded, set down the piece I'd been assembling, and turned to face him.

Nika's face showed pure terror. I couldn't tell whether she was worried for me or just worried about being left on her own. Either way, I smiled at her, hoping that would be enough to put her at ease.

If only it had been enough to put myself at ease....

My heart had been hammering before, but now it felt like it was about ready to explode.

I couldn't understand why I was being pulled off the line. Was I in trouble for ratting the guy out earlier? Or had they noticed me helping Nika?

I wasn't being dragged away, though. Was it because I was a woman? Or because I didn't know what was coming? Or just because I wasn't throwing a fit like that guy had been?

So many questions flooding through my head, and not nearly enough answers for them.

The trainer led me out a side door and up a set of stairs. I tried to keep up the map in my head, but I was so exhausted, I could hardly think.

We finally stopped in front of a door, one that looked identical to all the others. After a few moments that felt more like hours, the door finally slid open, and the trainer gestured for me to go inside.

The moment I was through, the door slid shut behind me, leaving the trainer outside.

I didn't feel any more secure, though. There were four men in this room. One sat behind a desk, leaning forward with his elbows on it, hands linked together.

Another sat in front, leaning back, looking relaxed and pleased about something.

Something about his hands, the size and shape of them as they splayed loosely over the arms of the chair grabbed my attention.

Teasingly familiar...

But he wasn't the immediate threat. The two men standing behind the desk were.

Horg, the asswipe from the ship, leered at me. The other guy looked just as dirty, just as much trouble.

Void.

They both grinned at me, giving me a look that made my entire body tense. Something was definitely going on.

"Please, come in," the man at the desk said, his voice light and pleasant, far too excited.

I nodded, trying to force down the lump in my throat.

All four sets of eyes were on me. Horg and his

buddy were easy to read. The man behind the desk was harder. He was pleasant, almost friendly.

Which made no damn sense.

The last one... I tried to get a better look at him, but when I turned to face him, Horg snapped, "Keep your eyes down."

"Yes, sir," I repeated, immediately looking down at the floor. Part of me wanted to just glare at him, but I knew it wouldn't get me anywhere. If anything, it'd just make whatever was going on worse.

The two men standing both snickered.

"Have... have I done something wrong?" I asked, unable to just stand there and keep quiet while all four men stared at me. I didn't need to look up to know they all still had their eyes locked onto me. I could feel their gazes burning across my skin.

"Not at all," the man behind the desk said in his light, relaxed voice. If I hadn't been so on edge, it might've even been soothing.

As it was, it just made me even more nervous. "From what I've heard, you've been exemplary on the line already."

Then what in Void's name am I doing here?

I risked a glance up and watched as the man leaned forward, his lips curved up into an absent smile. "Since you've done such a fine job, we've got something else for you to do...." His eyes flicked over toward the man sitting next to me, the one who looked so familiar.

At his words, the two men standing laughed openly, my heart sinking as I scoured the smooth surface of the desk for a weapon, anything at all.

I could easily imagine what the 'job' was, just by the way they watched me.

And I wouldn't go down without a fight.

But before I even had a chance to come up with a plan, the man who'd been sitting in front of the desk stood up.

With a smooth motion, he had me tossed over his shoulder like I weighed no more than one of my pieces of tracery.

At my shriek, he slapped my ass with a broad hand, shocking me into silence.

"She may not be broken in yet," the man behind the desk chuckled. "Sure you don't want to pick another?"

Strong fingers dug into my thighs, pinning me in place.

"Not at all." A low laugh. "I like them with a little fight." His hand tightened, kneading my ass almost reflexively.

He strode away, flashes of the floor and his back bouncing in my limited vision as my fists drummed against him.

"I'll send someone for you for dinner," the man behind the desk called as we reached the door.

"Don't make it too soon," my captor answered, then we headed down the corridor with the ugly laughter of the men still ringing in my ears.

LORCAN

Control.

The word repeated in my head, a mantra against the heat of the squirming bundle over my shoulder.

Control.

My system burned, veins on fire at her scent, her nearness. The rage at their threat to her threatened to spark an inferno.

Calculate the risk.

But nothing came.

I turned my head towards Cintha's hip, the lush curves begging to be bitten, licked.

Madness.

This couldn't stand.

With one swift movement, I spun her off my shoulder, facing the wall as I pressed against her back.

"Keep fighting, little girl," I growled loudly enough for the cameras. Pressing against her, I buried my face into the halo of disarranged curls at her neck.

"Cintha," I whispered, and she froze beneath me.

Void, her scent.

"Fight me," I spoke low in the shell of her ear, then bit it. "But listen."

I pressed into the curve of her ass, for the cameras, only for the cameras. "You know me. I'll get you out. I'll keep you safe. But you have to help me."

"What do you want?" she whimpered, her voice small.

I groaned into her neck.

What I wanted was to kill every man on this station who'd looked at her. Leered at her.

Who'd put the fear in her voice.

What I was going to do...

was regain control.

"I need you to pretend," I ground out. "I'm not going to hurt you, but they can't know that."

A tiny nod, then her body stiffened under mine as she screamed and bucked.

Control.

I flipped her around, pinning her arms above her head while I ran one hand lazily down her body.

Her eyes widened as we locked gazes, something far too close to hope sparking in her face.

The cosmetic work Doc had done before I left Orem would hold up.

Always had.

"Lorc--"

I fell on her lips with a bruising kiss, thrusting my tongue into her open mouth. Silencing her.

Tasting her.

Need and desire twisting until she relaxed in my grip.

"We'll finish this in my room," I growled, lifting her limp and dazed body.

Probably cradling it too gently, if someone was watching our little show.

But damned if I cared right now.

As I stalked down the corridor, she came back to life, squirming and kicking in my arms, thumping my chest with those small fists.

I tightened my grip on her legs and kept walking, but risked a glance down as we turned the final corner.

Was that a tiny wink?

I didn't believe in hope. I didn't believe in luck.

Doc had made sure we made our own luck by working hard, fighting hard, being smarter than the enemy.

If Brayden knew he had a woman I cared about

locked away in his facility? He'd own me. I'd have no choice but to scrub the mission, to either take her and flee or to just kill him right then and there. Neither of those were particularly good options.

The Cintha that I'd started to know back on Orem must have taken risks.

And for now, I'd have to gamble she'd be willing to take a risk with me.

I threw her on the bed, and sealed the door behind me as she scrambled away.

Her beautiful face was marred. I fought to smother a growl. No point in scaring her, but they'd pay. I'd make sure of it. Her eyes were still fixed on mine, not searching the room.

That was good, right? She'd been willing to fight before, had been looking for a weapon when surrounded by those assholes.

If she wasn't looking for a weapon now, please Void, let that mean she trusted me.

I flicked my eyes to the camera in the wall and then back again, willing her to follow my gaze, even as I slowly unbuttoned my shirt, draping it carefully over the back of the chair.

"There's no getting away, girlie."

A flash of comprehension and a tiny, almost imperceptible, nod.

"If you put on a good show for me, I'll tell your

boss," I leered as I stepped out of my pants. "Maybe he'll give you to me for keeps, as a sweetener for the deal."

Another flick of the eyes at the camera, then her chin raised, strong, defiant. "Not a chance, fucker. You want me, come and take me."

She spun, running for the door. The urge to chase, to hunt sang through my blood as I grabbed her around the waist, flinging her back to the bed.

Heart pounding in my ears, I stalked over to her, straddled her body.

Leaned over her, breathing in the quick breaths. The pink triangle of her tongue darted out, riveting my attention to her lips.

The mission, the act, everything knotted as the scent hit me.

Arousal.

The reins of my control slowly shredded as I ripped open her shirt, paused for a fraction of a second to appreciate her curves.

When she arched her back, thrusting her breasts against my hand, she met my eyes.

Trust.

Whatever I wanted.

Whatever we needed to show the cameras.

Whatever the cocktail of fear and pleasure was pumping through her system, I needed to be in control.

And I'd earn that trust.

"I own this pretty body now," I snarled loudly, careful to only lightly trace around her nipples until she quivered beneath me. "You're Logan's now."

Mind racing, I tore her leggings off, her long legs tempting me to explore, kiss, lick, tease.

Later.

For now, nothing but brutality.

Eyes fixed on her shaking below me, I mentally ran through the angle of the bed, the camera covered, scanned for any other cameras lurking.

It would have to do.

I flipped her to her belly, grabbed a fistful of hair, and put my mouth back on her ear. "I'm sorry. It won't be what it seems."

I reared back, pulling her hips up slightly, angling my back carefully, then smacked her beautiful ass. "Who owns you?"

"Lo-"

Her voice cut off as I plunged forward, grazing her slick folds, but not penetrating.

"Logan owns you," as I pulled back, away from her intoxicating heat.

Another shove forward into the bedding, another smack on her cheek, until she screamed. "Logan! Logan owns me."

And even though I'd coached her to learn the alias, it stabbed at me.

We couldn't risk a slip up. Couldn't risk her calling me by my real name.

Even if that's what I wanted to hear from her lips as she came.

This had to end.

I pushed forward, grinding her into the sheets as I rode her ass until, with a shudder, she came, shouting and bucking against me, her scent flooding the room.

And as sick as I was, her wild cries sent me over the edge behind her in a crazed mockery of passion.

As she lay beneath me, spent and panting, I pulled myself together.

"Let's get you cleaned up," I grumbled, trying to force the concern from my voice, barely caring what the cameras picked up, but knowing both of our lives depended on it. "I'm sure there's time for another round before dinner, but you're a wreck."

She lay quiet in my arms as I carried her to the bathroom.

My gut knotted.

I'd done lots of things for a job. Infiltrated, killed men who trusted me. Left destruction in my wake.

But nothing had ever left me feeling this way.

Raw.

Sick.

Dirty.

I elbowed the sprayer on, tested the temperature

with my back before turning to let the water run over Cintha.

"I think it's safe to talk in here," I whispered.

She didn't respond.

Oh, Void. Had I broken her?

Gently I pushed the hair away from her face, cupped the curve of her cheek.

"I'm so sorry, Cintha. I'll find another way." There had to be a way to finish the mission, keep her safe, and not reveal any of my growing pile of secrets to Brayden and his men. "We won't do that again."

Slowly, she raised her eyes.

"What if I want to?"

CINTHA

For a man who had always held a core of danger, of mystery that I couldn't touch, Lorcan, no, Logan here, was easily shocked.

Maybe I was easily shocked, too, because I shouldn't have liked that.

Not nearly as much as I did.

"You can't mean that," he whispered, setting me on the floor of the sprayer as if I were made of the most delicate glass.

I thought about it as the water washed over me, calmed my racing heart.

Maybe it was the situation.

Maybe it was that he was hot as sin, even with this new face.

Maybe I'd just always had a thing for a bit of danger.

I stepped towards him, teased one finger down his stillhard cock. "Apparently I can."

The tiny lines of tightness around his eyes didn't ease.

Interesting.

I'd suspected from Loree's stories that the men in her new crowd were good guys, no matter what they looked like.

And it looked like our little show had really bothered Lorcan.

I rubbed my sore ass.

Logan.

"The situation is fucked up," I agreed as I reached to turn up the sprayer. It'd been a long time since my morning shower back on Orem.

Before the fight with Talley.

My stomach clenched. She'd be fine. She had to be fine. Zeek would have gotten her back to the shop.

She knew to bunker down, wait.

She was safer than I was, and for now, that would have to do.

Lorcan took the gel from me, rubbed down my back and sides, sending tiny sparks through my skin with every touch.

"I'm here to shut it down. All of it."

I turned to rinse, waiting for the rest.

"I need more access. Which means I need the trust

of the guy in charge. Brayden." He looked away again until I stepped toward him, lathering his chest.

"Which means you could use a partner about now."

"If they suspect we're working together, that you're not just a fucktoy," he spat out, "they'll use you as leverage. I won't put you at risk like that."

I tilted my head. "I've been kidnapped, beaten, threatened with rape, taunted with some mythical promotion, and sold. What about any of that sounds less risky?"

"Who?" he demanded.

"Really? That doesn't seem like what you're here for, is it?"

By the smoldering look, I didn't think he was listening, just planning terrible things to those who took me.

And while I wouldn't mind Horg being taught a lesson, if Lorcan could shut the entire operation down, it was worth putting up with a lot.

Even if we escaped, how long would it be until Talley or some other girl was captured, sold away like a piece of meat?

Sure, it wasn't likely that taking down these assholes would get rid of all the trafficking. But if it put a dent in things, if it made the decks even a bit safer, personal revenge would have to wait.

I stepped back into the circle of his arms, pressed against the hard length of him.

"Cintha, no," he growled.

"Don't you dare tell me what I can like or not," I hissed. "And don't think they won't be wondering why we've been in here for so long."

His eyes flashed with acknowledgement and heat.

With a swift movement, he slammed the sprayer off, twirling me away from him. A broad hand forced my back down, hinging me at the hips.

"Brace yourself on the wall," was the only warning he gave me before the first smack hit my ass.

One spank after another, the punishing rhythm a promise for what was to come.

I could still almost feel the girth of him as he'd teased me in the bedroom, and my core tensed, waiting.

He paused and I gasped as he kneaded my hot flesh, then trailed one thick finger across my slick folds.

Just the tip of his finger parted my lower lips, the intrusion enough that my knees weakened.

One arm snaked around my waist, holding me up, supporting me as slowly, tantalizingly, he dipped deeper inside me.

I squirmed against his grip, desperate and hungry.

The pounding at the door shot through us both like a splash of cold water.

Lorcan released me, and slowly, I slid down to my

knees, desperately trying to gather any threads of sanity I had left.

Were they watching us? Had they heard us, even over the water?

Lorcan's voice was tight, strained, as he called loud enough for me to hear, "Teldra, please come in."

A low, mocking laugh answered. "Am I interrupting anything?"

LORCAN

Opening the door to Teldra had me completely on edge.

It had been so easy to lose myself in Cintha, the silken touch of her skin, her beguiling responsiveness.

Control.

I'd nearly lost that with her, and now we were in even more danger than before.

Had they overheard what we'd been talking about in the shower? Was my cover blown? Would I have to take Cintha and fight our way out of here?

When Teldra walked in, she wrinkled her nose slightly then looked away, as if bored with the entire thing, not at all bothered by my barely dressed state.

"Since you were so taken with your new toy, Brayden asked me to prepare her to join us for dinner tonight." She cocked an eyebrow, finally staring straight at me. "Unless you've finished with her, or want a new amusement for the rest of your stay here?"

A snarl threatened to break free from my throat.

"No," I forced out, "I'll keep her." Grabbing a sheet from the bed, I stalked into the bathroom.

"Cover yourself," I snapped, but gently helped her stand, wrapped the sheet around her myself.

She rolled her eyes at me, saucy minx, then pulled away, making a grand entrance to the bedroom, stumbling and shaking to Teldra's side.

Teldra didn't look shocked at Cintha's state, but she didn't look suspicious, either. Just that same vague sense of irritation, hostility held barely in check, that she'd radiated from the beginning.

Maybe it was at me.

Maybe that was just her natural demeanor.

"Dinner will be in an hour," Teldra told me as she led Cintha from the room. "Someone will come by to collect you."

I nodded. "If someone could come by to change the bedding around then, it'd be much appreciated. We seem to have made quite a mess of these."

Cintha blushed while a faint scowl crossed Teldra's face.

I hated embarrassing Cintha like that, but I knew it would just help sell my cover a little bit more. And in something like this, every little bit counted. Durl and Horg no doubt habitually bragged about their conquests, willing or otherwise.

Even Brayden had seemed like that sort of man.

So I needed to be, as well.

Despite her annoyance, Teldra nodded. "Someone will take care of it while you are at dinner."

Without another word, she turned and walked down the hall, Cintha in tow. Clearly, she wasn't as amused by these antics as Brayden had been earlier.

Which just raised more and more questions in the back of my mind, questions I didn't quite have the time to figure out right then.

I had an hour until someone would be coming to collect me. Precious time to try to find an access point, anything I could use.

All the while knowing that the cameras positioned everywhere would be watching my every move. I'd need a good story, and a better read on Brayden's characters.

So far, the only place I'd been that seemed likely was the office where I'd met Brayden. There was obviously some sort of communications control from that location to the rest of the facility.

Not ideal, but it was a start.

And with luck, Brayden would be preparing for dinner, not finishing up some last-minute work.

I dressed swiftly, then waited a few moments until I could be sure Teldra and Cintha weren't just down the corridor any longer. I slipped out of the room and headed in the direction of the office, my footsteps completely silent on the pristine floors. There wouldn't be any way to hide from the cameras, but as long as I looked like I knew what I was doing, I doubted it'd raise too much suspicion.

This wasn't my first trek through a guarded complex, after all.

And considering the building housed one of the most illegal outfits in the Empire, other than the factory rooms where the workers were trained and housed, it was surprisingly unguarded. Was Brayden being cocky, figuring no one would be able to find his complex out here? Or was I missing something?

Something was off. Everything about the job seemed slightly askew, as if seen underwater.

I could wait, observe the situation for longer, see if time would reveal the flaw in the pattern.

Or the additional time would just leave more opportunities for my cover to be blown. No job was perfect. Someone capable of dreaming up the wholesale capture and sale of other humans while being as downright cheerful as Brayden, was likely not particularly stable.

I had the hospitality of the house now.

There were no guarantees how long that would last.

The door to the office wasn't even locked. For all I knew it wasn't where the real work was done, just meetings, but surely there would be something of use, some starting place for my search.

I slipped in without ever once having spotted someone else in the empty corridors, closing the door behind me.

The desk was empty, but even in the low light, I could see the sheen of where fingerpads had pressed the surface.

Not the pattern, of course, but it was a start. One smudged section stood to the side.

It could be locked to a particular set of fingerprints. That would be how I'd do it.

But right now, it was my only option.

I pressed it, and immediately the surface lit, a keyboard and display lit from underneath.

No password request.

And... no true access. Just a dumb terminal with limited connection to other computers on the local network.

I growled, balling my hands into fists and resisting the urge to smash the damned desk.

I flopped down into Brayden's chair and let out a sigh.

Of course it would be too easy to just find an actual

computer and upload the worm that would give Nixie access to these files.

She'd been working for months to get her way in, but we needed this one last connection to be made manually.

The chirpy little AI was frustrated, but no more than I was right now.

All I wanted was to get the worm in place, confirm connection, grab Cintha, and get the hell out of here.

Instead, it looked like we'd be here for at least another day or two until I could find an access point.

With a shake, I pulled myself together. The terminal here wasn't full access, but it still had some information. More than I had.

And while Doc had made sure our bodies were weapons, she'd also stressed that information could trump brute force.

It made sense for this terminal to have map access, since this would be where Brayden would meet with guests and clients. As proud as he was of the place, he'd want to show them the extent of his operation.

A few key clicks later and I had a map of the base in front of me.

I grinned at it, scanning for anything that might indicate computer access.

The place was massive, though, and the interface wasn't really designed for this kind of searching, especially from someone who didn't already know the layout of the complex.

Finally, I found what I'd been looking for. There was a decent-sized room labeled 'security', not terribly far from where I was.

Glancing at the time, I knew I wouldn't be able to get there before dinner, but it would definitely be feasible to sneak to it either later tonight or tomorrow to upload the worm. Hell, if I played my cards right, I might even be able to get Brayden to take me there himself.

I was grinning like a fool when the door to Brayden's office slid open again. My head flew up in time to see Brayden walking in like he owned the place.

Which he did.

Casually, I left the map open.

He'd be able to see what I'd accessed. Trying to hide it would be only more suspicious. I relaxed my fists, my entire body tense, waiting for Brayden to call for guards.

But he didn't.

"Find what you're looking for?" he asked, his tone casual. No doubt he'd been watching me from somewhere on a security feed.

Now to find out if the story I'd come up with would stand.

"Yup," I nodded at the desk. "Nice little system you have set up here."

His eyes narrowed slightly, but he didn't say anything. Nothing to do but carry on.

"Figured it would take the ladies longer to clean up, so thought it'd be a good time to get an overview of all the places we saw this afternoon," I explained. "Get a complete grip on it, as it were."

His face broke into a mischievous grin, like a teenaged boy dressed in a man's suit. "Not surprised your new friend might need some extra time," he laughed. "Don't worry, Teldra will get her all presentable. She's done it before."

He bounced over to the map. "So, did you figure it out?" He pointed at various rooms, tracing a path. "There's the three operations floors we visited first, worker quarters are underneath, and shipping and processing are here."

He stopped, fingers drumming. "Not everyone is as interested in the actual operation as you are, you know."

I softened my knees, prepared to lash out. I'd have to find where Teldra had taken Cintha, fight my way to the shuttle, find another--

"It's nice to have someone new to talk to about it."

Oh.

That was unexpected.

Brayden walked over and leaned against the conference table, still grinning at me. "It's rare in this line of work to find someone with actual intelligence, not just interest in moving the product, but how the entire process works."

Product. People.

Maybe he just didn't see the difference.

"Most of the people I work with barely have enough brains to do the tasks I assign to them. They're incapable of thinking for themselves, incapable of looking at the bigger picture."

I kept my eyes on him, letting all of my other senses extend out, waiting to see if this was all just part of a trap.

The moment I heard boots coming down the corridor, I'd be across the desk, my hands around Brayden's throat. If he thought I couldn't get over to him before guards got to me, then he would be in for quite the surprise.

"But not you," Brayden continued. "You've shown you have sense and guts from your meeting with Durl. It was the reason I decided meeting you in person was a good idea. You weren't going to bow down to one of my lackeys, which meant you'd fit right in in this business. You were more than just muscles, interested in more than just screwing your way through the women here, though I will say, you chose an excellent one for a test run."

Void, killing him would be a pleasure.

Instead, I fought back my rage and returned his smirk, nodding along with him, the tension slowly leaving my body as his words sunk in.

He wasn't upset at me for snooping around.

He was pleased by it, since apparently it meant I was more like him. That thought alone almost made me shudder.

But it helped solidify my cover, which was exactly what I needed right that moment. And anything that bought me safety, was good for Cintha, as well. I wasn't going to argue with his logic, no matter how flawed it was.

"My methods have allowed me to corner the market on cheap, disposable labor." He grinned broadly again, eyes bright. "They've allowed me to build up quite the business and make a tidy profit, as well."

I nodded. "You are most definitely the largest and most affordable in the business," I acknowledged. That was the whole reason I was here, after all. If things went according to plan, not only would we be able to shut him down for good, but we'd be able to track down all of his clients, take them down, and free all the captives, as well.

Probably not the result he had in mind from my visit, but that wasn't my problem.

"You know," he paused, making a show of thinking, "I'd be willing to license my methods to you, if you were interested. The Fringe is quite a large place. It's not like I can be the only game in town, you know?" His grin widened even more. He was much too excited about this, but I couldn't do anything other than play along.

"I would be interested in that." I forced my lips to mirror his smirk, rather than a snarl. "But I'll have even more questions about the entire process, from startup to training procedures - the whole works. You understand, I'm sure." However many questions it took to get access, I'd come up with them.

Brayden slapped me on the back, blissfully unaware of his proximity to my claws. "Absolutely! I can't wait to show you the rest of the operation. I'm sure we'll do great together."

As much as I needed to act as if this guy was a mastermind, I couldn't shake the feeling that he was a blundering idiot.

How had he gotten this far without the Empire shutting him down? There was definitely something more going on here.

I just had to figure out what it was.

CINTHA

Teldra walked at a brisk pace, forcing me to practically run to keep up with her.

Every once in a while, she glanced over her shoulder at me, as if to make sure I was still following. She needn't have bothered, since anyone could've heard me stumbling my way down the corridor.

"Did you have fun with Brayden's newest friend?" Teldra called back without looking. "Hopefully, he was at least a little more enjoyable than working on the line. It doesn't look like you're too marked up."

My face flushed at her implications.

It wasn't like I could tell her I really did enjoy my little tryst with Lorcan, even if it was faked for the cameras.

Her attitude was strange, the assumption that

Brayden and his friends would be more likely to abuse a sex partner than not, disturbing.

Not once did she slow her pace, leaving me struggling to catch up. I was still exhausted from having been on the assembly line all day.

And as much fun as being taken to Lorcan's room had been, it wasn't any more relaxing.

That shower did feel heavenly, especially with his naked, wet muscles only inches away from me the entire time.

Our little playtime afterwards, though... heat ran through me in a full body blush. Having been interrupted, just at that moment, meant I was wound tighter than ever.

When Teldra finally led me into another room, I just wanted to collapse. My entire body ached, my muscles all begging for some rest.

But Lorcan was relying on me, I chided myself. He needed a partner.

I scanned the room. Bigger than the guest room, more personal items displayed.

A small, intricately wrought sculpture caught my eye, the deep blue curves and swirls making it appear to dance on the display shelf.

The sight of something so lovely here in this barren compound struck me.

"It's beautiful," I nodded towards it. "Where did you

find it? Who's the artist?"

Teldra ran her eyes over its lines, almost as if surprised to see it. Maybe she'd seen it so often as to not even notice it anymore.

What a shame.

"I've had it since it was made." No pride of ownership sang through her voice. I'd have heard it, had heard it plenty of times in dealing with my clients. People who owned beautiful things usually loved them, wanted other people to admire them.

But there was nothing but emptiness in her.

"So, tell me about Logan," she said, turning to face me, dismissing the sculpture. Her arms were crossed in front of her chest, eyes wide open, appraising. "Was he rough with you? Gentle? There's something different about him, something I can't quite figure out."

My face flushed even deeper.

I didn't want to tell her anything about him, didn't want her to know those details about him, about us.

Lorcan was mine, I wanted to shout.

But in reality, he wasn't.

Sure, he'd been friendly enough to me back on Orem, and seemed to want to get me out of here, but that was just because he was a nice guy.

It was his mission.

There wasn't anything between us, not really.

"I wonder why he chose you." She ran her eyes up

and down me. "I mean, you're not hideous or anything, but you're not a trophy girl, either."

This time, when my cheeks flushed, it was out of anger rather than embarrassment. But then, as I stood there, staring down at the floor, I realized she was probably right.

I wasn't anything special, wasn't any different than any of the other women on the assembly line.

"I... I don't know why he chose me," I said, hoping if she heard the slight wavering of my voice, she'd assume it was because I was scared.

This room was probably bugged, too, so Brayden or one of his men were probably watching and listening to everything.

And despite Teldra's lack of aggression, I couldn't trust her.

She didn't seem to be here as a captive, so that meant she was working for the boss.

No different than Horg.

"You're from Orem Station, aren't you?"

I nodded. There was no point in denying it. No doubt Horg had told them where each of us had come from already.

Teldra snorted. "I think Logan operates out of there, too. Maybe he's seen you around before."

"I.... I doubt it...." My voice was cracking now.

She was getting way too close to the truth, and I

didn't want her to know Lorcan and I were connected in any way.

If word of that got back to Brayden, then he'd just use me as ammo against him. I couldn't risk being a hinderance to him. "I don't…. I don't think I've seen him before. I'd remember him, I'm sure."

"Yeah, I bet you would," Teldra said with another snort. She ran her eyes over me again, pursing her lips as she did so. Then she walked over and circled me, making my heart pound even harder. "Well, if you're what he's chosen, we'll have to make sure you're looking perfect for him."

She rolled her eyes. "It's what my darling brother expects, after all."

Brother?

Before I could question or object, she was stripping me naked.

My entire body flushed as she circled me again, examining me closer.

"No bruises to cover at least," she muttered. "That's a first."

I fought back the urge to cover myself. I wasn't ashamed of my body, but I also wasn't fond of having her eyes all over me like that, looking at me like I was a piece of meat.

It reminded me of the way Horg and Durl had looked at me, like they wanted to devour me.

I wished I was back in Lorcan's room, safe with him, then kicked myself.

I couldn't rely on him to keep me safe.

I wasn't some fragile little princess. I could handle myself, even now.

Get myself through this, back to Orem, back to Talley.

No matter what.

"I know just the thing!" Teldra said before practically skipping off toward a closet and flinging it open. Inside were more fine clothes than I'd ever seen in my life. It was tempting to just stand there and gawk, like I was still some street urchin who only ever dreamed of a synthsilk dress.

I had plenty of fine clothes back home.

Well, I had some.

Enough.

She pulled out a dress, then walked over to me and held it up in front of me. It was black and sleek, with a slit up the left leg.

It was gorgeous. I wanted to run my hands down the fabric, but I stopped myself from touching it. Even after the shower, my fingers were rough, covered with cuts from the assembly line.

Where Nika and the others still were. I couldn't forget them, no matter what.

As mercurial as Teldra's moods seemed to be, it was safer to wait a bit.

Luckily, Teldra had turned back to the closet. "Once they get a look at you in this, none of them will be thinking straight. It'll serve them right, too."

"How long have you been here?" I asked her at last, desperate to try and connect with this woman.

Maybe if I knew her story, I could empathize with her, could understand her.

Make her an ally.

Teldra held another dress in front of me, switched back and forth between the two, considering.

She looked contemplative, and I wondered what she was thinking about. The dress, or something else?

"Since the beginning," she said after a few moments. Then she tossed me the first dress and added "Here, put this on."

I quickly pulled the dress on while Teldra crossed the room again, searching for something.

She went back to the closet as I adjusted the dress on myself, feeling more than a little awkward wearing it. Just because I owned a few nice dresses didn't mean I liked wearing them often.

They were pretty, but I always felt awkward when I dressed up. Like I was still a little girl playing pretend, like everyone else would look at me and laugh.

Now, it wouldn't just be clients or random people seeing me like this.

It'd be Lorcan.

What would he think when I walked into the room, looking like a wannabe Upper?

After all, what he normally saw me in was my work attire, made to handle getting hot metals splashed against it.

Definitely not sexy, definitely not feminine.

When Teldra came back with a matching pair of heels, I thought I would die. Those were most definitely not my style. I'd be lucky if I managed to keep from breaking my neck.

Void, this dinner was starting to get more and more terrifying.

"Have... have you ever tried to leave?" I asked her, hoping talking would get my mind off the torture to come tonight.

I doubted it would work, but I had to at least try, right?

"Why would I want to do that?" Teldra scowled as she led me over to a chair and helped me put the heels on. "Wouldn't this be everything I've ever wanted?"

I blinked. Her tone confused me. If she was serious, she was the enemy. A part of everything going on around me.

But... if these rooms were bugged, could I trust

anything she said? If it was sarcasm, did that mean she didn't want to be here?

Was she planning on escaping? Or did she mean something else? I wanted to ask her, but the words got stuck in my throat. There was something about her that kept me on edge, confused me.

And I had too many questions already.

I kept quiet, letting Teldra focus on getting me ready for the dinner. Once the shoes were on, she began applying makeup, more than I ever bothered with.

Every once in a while, she'd mutter something under her breath, but I couldn't quite catch what she said.

I doubted I was meant to, anyway.

Once she was done, she brought me a small mirror.

I looked gorgeous, but at the same time, I didn't quite look like myself anymore. I wasn't sure how I felt about it, but Teldra looked satisfied, so I kept my mouth shut.

Then, she brought out a small box and opened it. Inside was a selection of some of the most beautiful necklaces I'd ever seen.

Instinctively, I reached out and ran my fingers along them, a sense of calm washing over me as I did.

"These are lovely," I breathed, any sense of caution swept away at the familiar beauty of fine work. "Exquisite."

Void, what I wouldn't have given to have been back in my shop right then, working with my jewelry, rather than getting all dressed up to go to dinner with a guy so far out of my league and a psychopathic kidnapper.

"Pretty, aren't they?" Teldra's voice was flat, as if the box was filled with trash.

All I could do was nod. They were exquisite pieces, each carefully crafted using only the finest materials.

"This one has a bit of a weakness in the chain." I gently prodded one of the twisted lengths with my fingertip.

"What do you mean?" She pulled the box back towards herself to examine it.

"Right there, see?"

She frowned. "It's barely noticeable. How do you see it?" For the first time her voice sounded honest. No overlays, no secrets.

"It's my job to pay attention," I answered, wishing there was something I could say right now that would reach her. Slowly, I moved her hand to the chain, turned it over in her palm. "Right there, you can see the beginnings of a fracture. Wearing it would put more stress on the closure." Flicking my eyes up, I met her gaze. "You'd risk losing the pendent, the prettiest part."

For a long moment, she said nothing.

"Well," she said suddenly, "we'll have to make a different plan then, won't we?"

There was definitely something going on with her, something I couldn't figure out.

It was bugging me, and I wished I had Lorcan here.

Not to have him protect me, but so I could talk to him, bounce ideas off him, and figure out what was going on.

Maybe he'd have some more insight into her, since he obviously knew who she was. If only we had somewhere we could talk other than in the shower. Because, at this rate, we were going to end up taking quite a few showers.

Not that I quite minded that prospect. The more time I spent naked and pressed up tight against Lorcan's body, the better. Just the thought of it was enough to make my cheeks heat again.

Thankfully, Teldra couldn't tell beneath the layer of makeup she'd put on me. Otherwise, I had no doubt it would lead to another bout of sarcasm and jabbing remarks.

Teldra took the box of necklaces from me and picked two out of it. She held them up against my chest, the metal cool against the tops of my breasts. This dress didn't leave much to the imagination, and the necklaces would only help draw attention to my body.

But they were gorgeous, so I didn't really mind.

When I got back to the shop, I vowed to make myself something pretty to wear once in a while. It might not be nearly as extravagant as the necklace Teldra was fastening around my neck, with its deep green gems inlaid throughout it, but I'd be able to make it my own.

Focus on the details, that'd always been my strong point.

See beauty where I could.

Make it my own.

"There," Teldra said, standing back with her hands on her hips. She grinned now, mischievous, wolf-like. "The gems bring out the green in your eyes. The men aren't going to be able to keep their hands off you tonight."

Unless the man involved was Lorcan, I didn't want any of those grubby hands coming near me. Just the thought of Horg or Durl touching me made me want to gag.

Then Teldra leaned in close. "Maybe if you do a good job pleasing Logan, Brayden will move you off the assembly line, make you one of his permanent pleasure-women."

I shuddered at the thought, but either Teldra didn't notice or she didn't care.

Hell, for all I knew, that was the reaction she wanted out of me.

As much as I hated to admit it, I'd rather work myself to death on the assembly lines than spread my legs for whatever creep Brayden was trying to impress that week.

But with any luck, Lorcan and I wouldn't be here long enough to find out. At least, I really, really hoped so.

LORCAN

The entire walk to the dining area, Brayden continued to boast about his operation.

I tuned most of it out, since it wasn't any actual information.

He was like a sleazy salesman, trying to convince me to buy into his scheme, even though I'd already told him I was interested.

He seemed incapable of doing anything other than bragging about himself, though, and he'd turned it into an art form where he could spend hours going on and on without revealing anything.

If I hadn't already known better, I'd have sworn it was all a sham, that he didn't actually know anything or have a criminal empire. Men who talked this much without really saying anything tended to be full of hot air, reigning from the corner of some seedy bar, filling the air with tall tales and grand ideas.

Was the same true for Brayden? Was someone else pulling the strings, using him as a front man?

We were the first to arrive in the dining area he'd had set up. There were a handful of servants in the room when we arrived, two of them rushing forward to get us seated.

Normally, I'd have thought such a thing was just pretentious.

But I knew these weren't just regular servants, they were slaves, kidnapped from their homes and brainwashed into being his mindless servants.

I was good at my job, but damn did I hate parts of it.

When the door opened again, I sat up in my chair and had to suppress a groan as Cintha walked in.

When she'd left my room, she'd been beautiful, a woman I'd had my eye on for so long, finally within my grasp.

Now it was like she'd been transformed into some ancient goddess from one of Doc's history vids.

My breath caught in my throat as she stepped into the room, the dress and heels making her legs look absolutely lickable.

Void, there wasn't an inch of her body I didn't want to caress.

But this wasn't the time.

Instead, I stood and offered her my hand when she approached, helping her sit. "You look fabulous," I told her, acting every bit the gentleman.

I may have been using her for my cover, but I wasn't Horg or Durl.

Besides, Brayden would be looking for signs that I wasn't just another brainless idiot, like the men he usually worked with.

I needed to sell myself as being something more than them, something better than them.

I looked over at Teldra, who'd already seated herself at Brayden's left, and smiled at her. "Thank you for your help getting Cintha ready this evening. I appreciate it."

Teldra nodded curtly, looking as bored as ever sitting at this table.

"Dinner should be ready shortly," one of the servants announced, her pleasant voice ringing through the room.

Brayden nodded and grinned. "It'll just be the four of us tonight. Horg and Durl have other things with which to occupy themselves."

The look on Teldra's face told me she felt the same way about her brother's helpers as I did.

Especially since I had a good notion of what those two would find amusing.

Cintha had shuddered when Durl spoke earlier. Clearly, she knew what sort of man he was, too.

She'd hinted about something happening on the way here, but she hadn't given any details.

I could use my imagination, though.

Luckily, there was always room for a slightly higher body count on a mission like this.

"So, Logan, have you considered where you might like to set up shop?" Brayden asked, turning the conversation right back to business.

I should've expected it, but I'd hoped for at least a few moments where everything didn't have to revolve around him and his ideas.

Judging by the way Teldra rolled her eyes, she thought the same thing.

I couldn't quite figure his sister out, but I could already tell she had more intelligence than he did. Maybe she was the reason he hadn't gotten raided by the Empire.

"I haven't," I told him honestly. Because other than stringing him along, it wasn't going to happen. But he didn't need to know that. Not yet. "It's something that will take care and time to figure out. I'd hate to rush into anything. I'm sure you understand."

Brayden nodded, but considering he kept talking, I doubted he really did. "I've scoped out a few different places around the Fringe, places far enough from here that we wouldn't be in direct competition with each other. Remote enough to be ignored by the Empire, yet close enough to do business and find new resources."

Fighting back a sigh, I nodded and pretended to be interested in everything Brayden said. He droned on and on about each different location, extolling their virtues.

Cintha must have sensed my mounting tension. She placed her hand on my leg beneath the table, just the lightest of touches.

And everything else disappeared.

Control.

Calculation.

So long as I had her by my side, I could stay focused, could remember the mission at hand.

No matter what Brayden said or how much he tried to drive me insane, I could do this if I focused on Cintha, used her to remind me of everything at stake here.

As the servants brought out plates, Cintha's stomach rumbled, quiet enough that I was probably the only one who heard it. Still, I had a feeling if she wasn't wearing makeup, I'd have seen her blush.

Void knew when she'd last had a good meal.

Another debt they'd all have to pay.

I examined the women who brought in platter after platter of food.

They smiled.

Not in the fearful, teeth baring way I'd expected of captives and hostages, willing to do whatever they were told in order to avoid another beating.

These were genuine smiles, they giggled and whispered to each other as they passed by the door.

Something else to solve.

Maybe it wouldn't matter once we had all of Brayden's records, Nixie and Doc between them could certainly figure out what had been done to these women, what leverage had been used against them to accept their lives here so easily.

Cintha watched them, too, a small frown marring her perfect features.

I shot her a questioning look but she shook her head, her cloud of hair falling to hide her face.

I'd ask her later.

In the shower.

I realized I'd completely lost track of whatever Brayden was rambling on about and fought back a smile.

Even if it was completely inappropriate to whatever sales pitch he was driving home now, he wouldn't notice.

His sister might.

But the thought of Cintha in the shower, her lush

curves against pressed my body, bent before me, was enough to keep my mind distracted.

Too distracted.

But certainly worth it.

She tapped the side of my leg sharply and I rapidly brought my attention back to the table.

"You've barely touched your ciffo," Brayden exclaimed. "Never sure if I trust a man who won't drink with me, and this is the best on the market, or off."

He grinned, surely thinking this was how business was done.

But that was fine.

"You've given me a lot to think about," I countered. "I'll need to make sure my head is clear if I'm going to keep up with you."

I took a sip of the deep amber liquid. Not fantastic. Certainly not the best.

Whoever was doing the shopping for the compound was probably gouging him, running up bills for finer liquor knowing that this idiot would never know the difference.

Corruption all the way down.

I took another sip, then knocked of the rest back. "I could get a taste for this." I grinned, remembering at the last moment to keep it friendly.

Human.

Brayden smiled, waved his hands until the giggling women appeared to refill our glasses.

Neither Cintha or Teldra touched theirs. But he didn't seem to notice, just ran his hand up the thigh of the serving woman next to him.

For just a moment, the woman's eyes froze, almost as if she didn't recognize where she was.

Then the look was gone, so fast I would have thought I'd imagined it.

But I hadn't.

She smiled, twirled away, the short skirt fluttering around her hips.

Another pair of women came out and cleared the plates.

Brayden waved to an empty area of the room.

"I'd arranged a little bit of entertainment for us. An example of how well our training works." Excitement, bright and cruel, dripped from his words.

Teldra finally stirred herself. "Why don't I take the toy back, get her fitted up with more wardrobe." She raised an eyebrow. "She'll need more things if he's going to be keeping her."

The toy.

Control.

Whatever was happening to my control, it couldn't be the ciffo.

And it couldn't have just been the casual words. But I was more than willing to go to war for them.

Control.

Brayden waved his sister off until she subsided in her chair.

"Let the man keep her." He snickered, attempted, but failed, a whisper. "The way he's looking at her, she won't need much to wear anyhow."

"I'd prefer she stays," I carefully slurred my words as I sipped more of the disgusting liquor.

Highly developed senses weren't always a blessing.

"Good, good," Brayden rose from his chair, obviously oblivious to his sister's annoyance. "We're about to start, anyway."

He led us to a half-circle of padded chairs and I pulled Cintha to my lap, letting one hand idly roam across the silken skin the long slit of the dress exposed.

She stiffened. Either a good actress or truly annoyed.

It worked for us, either way, and I'd apologize later.

Even if the contact with her was the only thing keeping me focused.

The damn women showed up again, refilling our drinks.

"You'll like this," Brayden's voice was slurring heavily now, the words tripping over themselves. "A great example of the process." He slammed his drink down, waved for another.

I sighed. Did the same.

A pair of young men came through the opposite set of doors.

Half stripped to the waist, they looked reasonably strong, fit.

Like the women, they showed no fear, no signs of cowed or broken spirits.

One slapped the other on the back. From across the room I could hear them, voices light and teasing.

Whatever was coming, they weren't dreading it.

"I told you we'd work up to this," the dark-haired one said.

"Yeah, but I'm taking the prize this round," the lighter-haired one answered, lightly hitting the other on the shoulder. "My stats are way better than yours."

Stats.

Prize.

None of it made sense.

As the two reached the center of the cleared space, a chime reverberated through the room and they immediately struck antiquated, sloppy, fighting poses.

And at the next chime, they began to tear each other apart.

CINTHA

I couldn't stop shaking.

We staggered back to Lorcan's room.

Our room now, I supposed, but instead of the plain gray walls of the corridors, all I could see was blood.

His arm tightened around my shoulders. "It'll be alright, babe, I promise," he slurred.

How could he have sat there, watched those poor men batter each other, laughing all the while?

And now, it didn't seem to have affected him at all.

It must've been the drink.

I pulled away slightly, but he tugged me back to him as we turned the corner into the room.

I hated drunks. Buzzheads.

The thrill of losing control, losing myself into some chemical haze, had always seemed abhorrent to me.

It certainly hadn't helped my brother.

I'd thought better of Lorcan.

The lights flicked on in the room as soon as we stepped in.

I paused.

Three short stacks of fabric lay neatly folded on the built-in desk on the far side of the bed.

I slipped out from under Lorcan's arm and went to examine them.

Teldra's doing, no doubt.

Skirts and tops, more revealing than I would've preferred, but still, they'd fit.

It was almost thoughtful of her.

I frowned, remembering how she'd tried to get me out of the room before those men...

No, I didn't want to think about it. Couldn't think about it.

Lorcan came up behind me, slapped my ass half-heartedly. Earlier, that would have sent fire through my veins.

But now, now I didn't know how to respond.

"Go get yourself cleaned up, babe. I'll be waiting for you."

Joy.

In the shower I scrubbed the layers of makeup off, letting my gaze glide over that bit of wall that I'd pressed into just hours before, desperate for his touch.

I paused, slowly drying myself.

One thin wall away, he lay there, waiting for me.

How much did I really know about him?

Which Lorcan was real?

I swallowed, throat tight.

I wouldn't find any answers hiding in here like a child.

But when I worked myself up to slide open the door, I nearly laughed at myself.

Low snores greeted me from the darkened room.

I slid under the sheets, back to his, but he immediately rolled, wrapping his muscled arm around my waist, pulling me back against his groin.

Oh.

Whatever else the drink had done to him, surprisingly it hadn't done anything to soften...that.

I wriggled, trying to get away from the hard length, but his arm kept me still like a vise.

"Cintha," he hissed, only barely loud enough for me to hear. "Stop moving."

At his command in crisp, un-slurred words, I froze.

"I'm trying to give you an excuse to get a good night's sleep," he continued softly. "But that," he punctuated his words with a sharp rock of his hips, pressing into my ass, "isn't helping. So, try not to make things more difficult, will you?"

He wasn't drunk.

At all.

That didn't make any sense.

I'd seen what even a couple glasses of ciffo did to people.

Not the good stuff, certainly. Not down in the Under.

But every now and then, a shipment would get 'misplaced', rerouted from the intended recipients up-station.

It might be a snooty liqueur, but it didn't take much before even strong men were blithering idiots.

"What's going on?" I hissed back, suddenly desperate to see his face. "How are you not totally wasted?"

The snoring continued, but now that I was paying attention, it wasn't from right behind me.

A recording.

I bit back a giggle. So, our options were we could talk in the shower, or in bed with the lights out?

That would be productive.

"My stomach's not happy with me," he grumbled softly. "But as for the rest..." He sighed. "I promise I'll explain everything if we get back to Orem. When we get back,"

he corrected himself. "There's a lot you don't know about me. Us. I'll explain it all."

A long pause.

"Can you trust me?"

He waited, the words heavy in the air between us.

I didn't know what choice I had, but that wasn't the answer he was waiting for.

It wasn't the answer I wanted to give him.

He pressed on. "No matter what you see? No matter what I do?"

The undercurrent of tension between us brought the scene of the fight before me again, the two men who had seemed so friendly.

The lighter-haired one still grinning, laughing, as he beat the head of his friend into a bloodied pulp before us.

Every muscle in my body knotted.

Lorcan's arm loosened around my waist, large hand running up and down my side, soothing, relaxing, as if trying to calm a wild animal.

"I don't understand," I whispered. "How they could do that, how he could have..."

The worst part, the absolutely worst part, was when the victor had been led away from the remains of his friend.

And he'd called over his shoulder. See you next time, he'd said.

No remorse, no regret.

Almost no comprehension.

"I don't know, but I'm going to find out," Lorcan promised, bringing me back to the here and now. "Let me tell you what I found while you were getting dressed."

My chest tightened as he told me of finding the map, of Brayden discovering him in the office.

"But it doesn't make any sense," I argued. "Why wouldn't he care?"

"I don't know. We have to assume everything here is captured on the security cameras." He pressed his forehead against my head. "But I've got to get into the control room. Got to get into their computers."

I didn't understand why. And I didn't care.

Concrete steps.

I could handle concrete, achievable steps.

"Tell me the directions again."

He repeated them, and again and again, until we both knew how to get there from the few places we'd been to in the complex.

Now to come up with a way to reach it under the watching eyes of the cameras.

He pressed a kiss to the back of my neck and my skin flared.

"It's enough for tonight, love." He tossed his arm back over my waist, loosely now, but still as comforting, as possessive.

Love. He couldn't have meant that.

Just a phrase. A random endearment.

Like babe. He probably said it to all the women.

A word. Nothing more. Nothing real between us.

"You need a good night's sleep," he murmured, no doubt writing off my tension as a result of our situation. Which was enough to worry about, I reminded myself. "We'll figure it out in the morning."

And though I would've sworn my mind wouldn't stop racing all night, pounding on the door jolted me awake.

"Boss wants to see you for breakfast," Horg shouted. "He's waiting."

Despite myself, I curled away from the sound of his voice, clutched the sheet closer around me.

Lorcan sat at the edge of the bed, fully dressed, eyes narrowed.

"Anything you want to tell me about?" he asked, tone mild, but even I could pick up the scent of violence in his words.

"No," I whispered and grabbed an outfit without meeting his eyes.

Something could easily have happened back on the shuttle that brought us here.

It was something between luck and a miracle that it hadn't.

But I still didn't want to talk about it.

We arrived back at the same dining room, all traces of blood washed away, but still, I couldn't look.

Lorcan seated me where he had been the night

before, ensuring my back was to what now seemed a haunted room.

Brayden slouched in the chair opposite me, running a hand through disheveled hair. Skin reddened and eyes puffy, the ciffo had certainly done him no good.

"Let's finalize that deal today," he mumbled over a bite of sweet fruit brought out by yet another round of smiling, happy women.

I thought of Nika, struggling on the assembly line.

What would it take for her to be moved up here?

Was the price worth it?

While Lorcan dealt with Brayden, Teldra caught my eye.

"Sounds like you'll be attached to our visitor for a while," she commented as she sipped her kaf. "He might buy you, but chances are he'll move on."

For a moment, I thought I saw a flicker of understanding, of concern, across her face.

"I, I wouldn't know what his plans are," I mumbled, the delicate fruit turning to ashes in my mouth.

"Well, we never do, do we?"

Always it seemed like she was saying something underneath her actual words. Something that if I were smarter, faster, I could grasp.

"Either way," she continued, "it wouldn't hurt for you to have a better sense of where things are in the compound."

She glanced across at her brother. "They could be days hashing out the details. Or," she shrugged, all traces of empathy or sympathy gone, "get the deal done tonight and you'll be bounced back to play with the rest of the boys."

Teldra shrugged, popping another piece of fruit into her mouth. "Who knows?" She pushed back her chair, rising and grabbing my wrist.

"You men go play with your empires. We're going for a walk."

And before I could get a word in, she swept out, pulling me behind her.

Once again, she didn't talk, just led me through the labyrinth of corridors. I tried to catalog each turning and each branch, compare it against the map Lorcan had whispered to me last night, but my thoughts kept distracting me.

Would we go and look over the assembly lines?

Maybe see where the young fighters from last night had come from?

Instead, Teldra surprised me again. We arrived in a small room, a few low chairs scattered throughout, but no one else inside.

"I need to think," she muttered. With that, she slapped the panel by the door. It sealed, and a rumbling noise began.

"May as well sit down and enjoy the show." She

sprawled in one of the low chairs, eyes fixed on the wall before us.

I sat next to her, wondering what I could say, what I could do, that would reach her.

"What's going on?" I whispered.

For long moments she didn't answer.

And then I gasped, my question forgotten, finally realizing what she was watching.

The wall before us irised open, heavy permasteel slowly pulling back to reveal a brilliant expanse of stars.

Despite everything, I couldn't help but walk to the plexi, press my hand against it, overwhelmed by the velvet blackness before us, the tiny pricks of light all there was to remind me of a world outside this place.

And somewhere out there, Talley was waiting. I had to get back home.

"Sometimes it's important to just watch it go by, wait for the right moment," Teldra finally said.

And no matter what I asked, she refused to say anything further.

I was beginning to regret not having eaten more breakfast when she suddenly stood.

"We should be getting back."

For once, she didn't race in front of me.

"What did you do, before here," she asked as we walked side-by-side through the corridors.

"I was, I am a jeweler. I make things of my own

design, sometimes for client commissions." As I spoke, I could almost see my shop, feel my tools in my hands.

"Any family?"

"I have a niece," I smiled, despite myself. "She's hit those difficult years, but we'll get through them. Just as soon as I get back."

I shot a glance towards Teldra, but she didn't react.

"Where's her own mother?" she pressed.

"Long gone. And my brother, well, he's never been around much."

"Brothers are," Teldra smiled, "problematic sometimes."

As ridiculous as the comparison was, her idiot, slave-trafficking sibling and my absent, buzz-headed one didn't seem that far apart.

Just for the moment.

She paused before we re-entered the dining room.

"Good luck." It sounded like she meant the words. I just wished I knew what she was talking about.

Lorcan and Brayden were already at the table. For all I knew, they'd stayed there talking about their stupid deal.

I didn't understand how Lorcan put up with Brayden's inane jabbering, but that wasn't my job.

I ran over the route to the office again, added the corridor doors and lifts that Teldra and I had gone down on the way to the viewing room.

Maybe, maybe...

Lorcan stood as we entered, a slightly raised eyebrow his only indication of concern.

And why should he worry?

In what was becoming a maddening routine, like a nightmare we couldn't wake from, the smiling women came, brought more food, and then finally, something different happened.

Horg burst in.

"Durl's dead."

LORCAN

Crap.

Horg stood still, arms crossed over his chest, glaring straight at me.

If my cover had been blown, I was going to be pissed if it was because of that asshole's murder. Sure, I'd thought about it.

Lots, even.

But I hadn't, not yet.

I reached beneath the table, taking Cintha's hand in mine. Her fear spiced the air. I rubbed my thumb over the back of her hand, hoping she'd understand.

She'd be safe, no matter what.

Brayden knocked over his chair as he jumped up, stumbling back, his eyes wide.

"What do you mean?" he stuttered.

For the last three hours, he'd barely strong two coherent words together.

He certainly wasn't going to be up to this particular challenge.

"Routine sweep found him behind supply crates in the shuttle bay," Horg snarled, still watching me.

Some ancient military wisdom that Doc had drilled into us seemed reasonable about now.

Offense, defense, blah blah.

I pounded my fist on the table. "What sort of operation are you running here?" I shouted. "How do you expect me to trust you with my business, consider being an investor in this rinky-dink operation, if you can't even keep your own compound secure?"

Brayden's head swiveled like it was on a stick, caught between my accusations and Horg's glare.

"We're safe," he assured me, face reddening. "It's always been safe here, we've never had a problem."

"A surprise dead man sure seems like a problem to me." I raised my eyebrows, waiting for some excuse. And any more data. That'd be useful right about now.

Brayden threw his glass at the wall. "What's on the camera feeds," he demanded shrilly.

Irritation flared across Horg's face. "Wiped. Everything that would've given us any information from last night."

Cintha stiffened next to me.

Dammit.

I stood, pulled her to me. "But we're certainly not going to be finalizing any business arrangement while you've got this catastrophe hanging over you."

I wrapped my arm around her shoulders, tucking her in to me. So small, so fragile.

"Yes, yes," Brayden replied, flustered. "We'll get this solved, it must've been an accident."

"I would certainly hope so," I snapped back. "It's not as if it was some random worker. I would've thought that your trusted men, at least, would've been safe here. Now I'm beginning to wonder about your priorities."

"No," he exclaimed. "There's no problem at all. Why don't the two of you go, have a little fun. Let me know if you need another girl, maybe a few more?" His eyes were wild, searching the room as if there were answers to be found on the walls. "We'll let you know when we can get back on track. I'm sure there's nothing to it. Just a little accident."

"We'll see." I stomped out of the room, Cintha silent at my side.

In the corridor, I headed back towards our room, but she pulled me to a stop, moved my hand to her shoulder and stepped back, making it look like I was shoving her against the corridor wall.

My smart, smart lady.

"Did you, did you kill that man?" she whispered into my chest.

Void. Maybe too smart.

"I didn't, I swear to you," I whispered back, pushing against her, playing for the cameras. "Cintha, I can't promise that no one's going to get hurt. But I'll never lie to you. I didn't do this."

She swallowed, nodded. "I understand, I just..."

She didn't have to say anything. The fight, that travesty of after-dinner entertainment that Brayden had staged last night, had been disgusting.

And yes, I was well aware of the irony of someone with my proclivities being disturbed at a display of violence.

But those men, there was something wrong. They took none of it seriously, even at the end.

Even I knew there were consequences.

And whatever Cintha had gone through in life, that level of violence had upset her, rocked her to her core.

She'd always be safe with me, no matter what she saw, no matter what happened around her. I'd just have to make sure she knew it.

"I have a plan," she murmured as she wiggled against me, blurring my good intentions as my blood raced towards my cock.

"I'm all yours, I mean, all ears," I hastily corrected.

Luckily, she didn't notice my slip.

"Do you have whatever you need for the computer room?" she moaned breathily as I ran my fingers over the side of her breast, pinching the hardened nub, rolling it between my fingers until she gasped.

"Always." I buried my face in her neck, waiting for her next move.

Her panting gasps pressed her chest against mine, pulling my focus until the world revolved around her.

Only her.

So, when she shoved me away, I stumbled back, unprepared.

"Then you better catch me, but not too fast." Her grin was wicked, intoxicating.

Addicting.

And with a stinging slap against my cheek, she sprung away, racing down the hall.

CINTHA

That might've been the stupidest thing I've ever done in my life.

Tearing myself away from Lorcan had been hard enough, but teasing him, taunting him, that was madness.

I tore down the hallway, reaching out for the corner to slingshot myself at the turn.

His surprise had bought me a few seconds' lead, nothing more. But I wasted one of those precious seconds to kick off the damn heels.

If we were to have any chance at making this look real, I'd need every advantage I could get.

Was it at this left? No, the next.

"You're going to be sorry when I catch you." The growl behind me sent a thrill through my veins.

I spurred ahead, drawing on every memory of outrunning the gangs back on Orem, back in the stations between there and the orphanage that Loree, Daix, and I had broken out of.

Lungs sobbing for air as I ran, I frantically tried to remember the map, the way to the observation room Teldra had showed me, my best guess as to how to end up at that office.

And all the while, I had to figure out how to stretch this out, twist and turn until anyone looking through the security cameras assumed they knew exactly what we were doing, what scene was going to be repeated, and lost interest.

Lorcan certainly hadn't.

I was fast, I'd had to be.

But I knew he was faster.

As I ricocheted around another turn, the tips of his fingers grazed against the fabric of my skirt.

I spun, twisting out of his grip, and dodged again.

And he growled behind me.

Not a curse, not a threat, but a deep rumble, heavy with promise.

Almost there.

Void, I hoped I'd remembered correctly, but my mind couldn't focus, couldn't grip anything other than the need to run.

I broke into a darkened empty room.

This should be it, this should be where...

"Got you."

All of my thoughts scattered as he tackled me, wrapping me in his embrace, protecting me as we rolled on the floor.

His elbows to either side of me, I was pinned beneath him.

Helpless.

At his mercy.

"So smart," he whispered, grinding his hard length into my core, sending a burst of pleasure spiraling through me despite the layers of fabric between us.

With infinite care, he pulled my hair away from the shell of my ear and nipped at the ridge until I squirmed beneath him.

"So brilliant, to get us here,." His tongue darted out and a low moan escaped my lips. "But we might have a problem, love."

"What?" I panted, unable to breathe, unable to think, to do anything but feel. "What problem?"

"I don't think I can fake it this time," he admitted. "We have to stop now or I--"

I turned my head until my lips brushed his neck. "What if I said that's all right?"

Under my lips I felt him swallow hard.

And again.

"You don't have to trade your safety with that," he

finally managed. "You deserve better. You should have better."

Better?

Better than this strange, bewildering man with the threat of violence and danger hovering barely contained under his skin?

With his mysteries and questions and mission.

His touch that destroyed me, brought out desires and needs I'd never acknowledged.

"You wanted me to trust you," I whispered. "Trust me."

He stiffened above me.

"I want this. I want you."

I bit the curve of his neck at the shoulder, what was meant to be a playfulness turning into something harder.

Hungrier.

And that growl came again, rumbled through him, the sound alone enough to make me wild.

"Come and get me," I repeated. "But this time, mean it."

With a quick flip of my hip, I twisted beneath him, scrambling to my hands and knees to crawl away.

"Not happening, love."

His hands wrapped around my hips, jerking me back towards him.

With a quick slash of his hand, he ripped through

my shirt, the fabric pooling down my arms, exposing my spine to his touch.

"You want this, do you?"

One hand cupped the back of my head, holding me still, while his other slowly traced up my calf and drew patterns on the inside of my knee.

Then waited at the edge of my inner thigh, just beneath my skirt.

"Be still, then," he commanded, and every fiber in my body strained to obey him.

But he didn't play fair.

Who the hell would have guessed the skin of my back could be so sensitive?

But he kissed and bit and licked. Dropped random touches where I least expected it.

As long as I lay still, panting beneath his touch, his other hand crept up, ever so slowly towards my slick folds.

But the instant I squirmed, arched into his touch, beat my hands against the floor, his hand froze.

Now he was the one taunting, teasing.

Controlling.

And I loved it.

"Please," I begged him, near incoherent with want.

He flicked his fingers across the seam of my lower lips and I bucked, all interested in winning this little game long gone.

"As I recall," he started, and paused, and I froze, desperate for him to move again. "We were interrupted before, just as I was getting here."

We had been, and now I was wound just as tight as I'd been in the shower, bent over for him, his fingertip barely penetrating me.

"Should I keep going this time?"

"Please," I pleaded again.

One finger, back and forth, dragging through my heat until suddenly, he drove it inside me, pumping and twisting.

"Oh!" I yelped, any ability to stay still blasted away.

Another finger joined the first, and another, twisting and grinding inside me.

Nothing had ever felt like this, nothing had left me so open, so raw, every nerve ending exposed to his touch.

Smack!

I jolted at the sudden impact of his hand on my ass, so lost in sensation I hadn't even realized he was no longer holding me down but had moved to kneel between my legs.

One quick blow after the other, in time with the pumping at my core, and I shattered, stars exploding in my vision as I screamed.

LORCAN

Control.

Calculation.

Fuck that.

Cintha's bewitching perfume filled the air, fuel for the fire that burned through my veins.

Gently, I turned her over, cradling her to my chest as the aftershocks ran through her.

"I think I caught you fair and square," I murmured into her cloud of hair.

"We're done?" she asked in a small voice.

Minx.

Irresistible minx.

I lowered her back, her face staring up into the darkness of the room.

Never, not in any fight, not in any mission, had I

ever been so thankful for our enhanced vision.

Every curve of her body, every emotion that crossed her face, was visible to me. I licked one of the fingers that had been deep inside her.

"Later, I'll find more ways to make you scream," I promised.

"But for now," I grabbed her hips and thrust into her wet heat, sheathing myself in her to the hilt.

I froze, panting, head bowed at the sensations, her tight body wrapped around my cock.

Nothing could feel better than this, nothing.

Then she flexed muscles deep inside, and I hissed.

"Come on," she gasped, "get me."

Driven to the edge of madness by the scent of her, the touch of her, the taste of her, I seized her hips and pounded, driving forward and pulling back until she writhed, impaled on my cock.

One arm wrapped around her hips, keeping her tight against me while I drove in and out, the other was now free to explore, to delight in her lush body.

"I am never, ever, letting you go." I drove into her harder with each word, possessed by my need for her.

Her eyes, hooded with pleasure, still betrayed a hint of doubt.

Given time, I'd fix that, assure her of my intentions.

But for now, I had a single mission.

Her.

With my free hand, I kneaded her breasts, circled her clit, until her breath came in shuddering gasps, her eyes widened, unfocused and dark.

Her low moans ripped into me, tearing at my control, until I finally, completely, snapped, driving into her until she cried out with pleasure and, roaring her name, I fell over the edge with her.

Heart pounding in my chest, for long moments I lay beside her, stroking her skin through the tatters of her shirt.

"When we get home," I whispered, "I think I'm going to have my work cut out keeping you in clothes."

She snuggled against me. "Maybe I just shouldn't wear them."

Her words went straight to my cock, eager for another round.

But we were here for a reason.

Well, another reason.

"Come on, love," I stood, reached down, and lifted her to her feet.

"Still a little wobbly, I see." Grinning, I picked her up and sat her on one of the three desks in the room.

In the darkness, she glowed before me.

Makeup smeared, hair everywhere, she looked more beautiful now than when Teldra brought her prettied and primped to the dinner.

"Here," I slid my shirt off and offered it to her.

She didn't reach for it, and I kicked myself. Of course, she couldn't see. I guided her hand to the sleeve and helped her fasten the buttons.

"Wait here for a minute, alright?"

I went back to the doorway, stuck my head out into the hall.

No one was coming. Hell, we'd both been loud enough that there was no question of what we've been doing.

Probably the entire compound was aware.

We should have a few minutes to work.

I looked around, but still found no proper terminals. Dammit.

"I'm going to turn on the light, watch your eyes. This has to be the right room."

I flicked on the panel to midway, more than enough for me to see every detail of the room, and enough for her not to feel lost in the dark.

I'd crossed half the room, stepping over the chairs we hadn't shoved to the side during our chase, when Cintha squeaked.

"What is it?" I rushed to her side.

She turned, burying her face against my chest, and I looked over her shoulder.

On the other side of the desk, wedged between it and the wall, was a very dead Horg.

At least, what was left of him.

CINTHA

Even with my face buried in Lorcan's hard chest, I could still see the remains of Horg. And my mind couldn't stop spinning.

"They must have come here right away, left when we did," I murmured.

While we'd been racing through the compound, twisting and turning through every corridor I knew, Horg and someone he trusted must have come straight here.

And then...

"Whoever it was must have been coming to check the cameras," Lorcan's arms tightened around me, holding me safe.

Nothing would hurt me while he was there.

And the killer was obviously long gone, otherwise we'd have already been attacked in the dark earlier.

Then, a realization hit me like a ton of bricks. Lorcan definitely couldn't have been the one who'd killed Horg.

And if he didn't kill Horg, then it made sense that he was telling the truth about not killing Durl.

I'd trusted him before out of instinct, but now I had proof of what he'd been saying.

At least, as much proof as I was going to get until the real killer was discovered.

"I need to check him for any clues, anything useful." Lorcan kissed me on the forehead one more time before crossing over to squat down next to the body.

I stood there, arms wrapped around my chest, and watched as he examined Horg. I should've been over there, should've been helping him, but I was rooted where I stood.

It was silly to be so scared of a dead body, but I couldn't quite convince myself to snap out of it. Instead, while Lorcan looked over the body, I scanned the rest of the room, looking for any other clues.

That's when I noticed it. The wall next to Horg, behind Lorcan, looked odd.

Out of place.

I couldn't quite figure out why it looked so different.

Then, it hit me.

It was probably some kind of secret door. Which would explain how Horg and his killer had gotten in here without us seeing them in the halls. The entire complex probably had secret doors and passageways scattered throughout it. Which would be why there was rarely anyone in the halls.

"Lor...Logan," I said, catching myself before saying his real name. For all I knew, they still had recording in this room. "Is that a door behind you?"

Lorcan looked over at me, brows furrowed, then followed my gaze. He stood and examined it for a moment, running his fingers all around the odd-looking area. He grinned, then glanced at me again. "Brilliant lady strikes again."

He went back over to the body, searching through the pockets. A few moments later, he stood back up with a keycard in hand. When he went back over to the wall, he slid his hand with the keycard through a hair-fine gap.

Moments later, the sound of mechanical locks could be heard disengaging before the door slid inward slightly.

Putting one finger to his lips, Lorcan motioned for me to keep quiet. Then, he slipped through the doorway and into the darkness on the other side.

I waited, holding my breath.

What I wouldn't have given to be back in my shop,

working with Talley. Listening to Talley whine as only young girls can.

I wanted to be back on Orem Station with my friends, back living the life I'd fought tooth and nail for.

The Under might not have been the safest place in the Empire, but it was mine, my home.

It wasn't some mysterious complex in the middle of nowhere.

Even in the Unders, if I yelled for help, there would always be people around, people I could trust to have my back. Here, the only person I had was Lorcan. No matter how loud I screamed, no one else would come to my rescue. Other than Lorcan, I was completely alone.

But as I stood there, staring at the doorway, I realized that didn't make me scared.

It made me angry. Angry at myself for getting into this mess.

Angry at Horg and his lackeys for kidnapping me.

Angry at Brayden and everyone who worked for him for organizing this bullshit.

No, I wasn't scared anymore. I was angry, pissed. I wanted answers and I wanted Brayden to rot in one of the Empire's prisons.

When Lorcan came back out, he was grinning. "Good job. That's exactly what we needed."

I stalked forward, following Lorcan into the dimly lit room.

It was filled with banks of computers and, for once, an obvious terminal.

"Does it have what you need?" I whispered. "How long will it take?"

If Horg was dead, if he'd been coming here, the murderer had to be someone high up. They couldn't call this an accident, not with half his face burned off by laser fire.

"Not long at all." Lorcan's teeth flashed in the low light, then his lips twisted. "You might want to look away, love."

"Why?" It stung, more than it should. "You need to do secret spy stuff?"

"No, I just don't want you upset."

But I wouldn't turn, too angry to care anymore.

With a sigh, he raised his left arm and, with the fingernail of the right, sliced the skin open.

Not exactly a fingernail, I realized.

Looking closely, it was more like a claw.

He pulled out a tiny package and opened it with his teeth to reveal a tiny pointed crystal.

Blood from the package stained his lips, pulling my focus until my brain kicked into gear.

A micro data-spike.

Of course.

I hurried around to his side of the console, pulling off the shirt to rip off one of the sleeves.

"Give me your arm," I fussed.

Fine. He might be terrifying, he might be some sort of secret agent.

But he was mine, and he was bleeding.

I could do something about that.

"What are you doing?" Computers, terminals, that wasn't my scene.

Loree, now there was a girl who could make the damn things sit up, dance, do anything she wanted.

I had always needed something I could see, work with, get my hands into.

Maybe I should've diversified a little.

"This," he said, as he slid the tiny crystal into a slot, "is a Nixie extension."

"What's a Nixie?"

He rolled his eyes and grinned. "That's a matter of some debate in the Pack, but Eris would insist she's not a what, but a who."

Eris. Another name I'd heard from Loree. A sister-in-law.

Void, how many sisters-in-law was I about to walk into? I liked my little family just fine, and wasn't always great with a lot of people, and...

I shook my head. That was presuming a lot, and this wasn't the time.

"Nixie is an AI, one of the smartest I've ever seen. Luckily for us, she's on our side." He shrugged. "Well, most of the time, until she gets bored. Then she does whatever the hell she wants."

He tapped the console. "Without us having the location for their systems, we couldn't break-in, we were working blind. We pinged off satellites, tried to trace communications, but nothing snapped."

"So, you brought her here? That doesn't sound safe." I frowned. "What if they'd found it? Her? Whatever."

"We took the chance that even if they'd taken my clothes and patted me down, they wouldn't find the chip."

My cheeks flamed. I'd certainly been wrapped in those arms and had never felt anything besides hard muscle.

And hard...

"That, well, um. So, she's on that one little chip?"

Good move Cintha, try not to think about what those strong arms had been doing just a few moments ago.

"No," he shook his head, tapping a few keys on the console. "Sort of like a stripped-down copy of her. Just enough to start working its way out of their systems, make a hole in their security, and find commwaves the signal can ride out on."

He leaned back. "Nixie's out there waiting. As soon as she has the signal, she'll be in here, grab their files, and the team can get to work." A vicious smile. "A coordinated strike should wrap them all up, Brayden, his clients, suppliers, victims. All of it."

When she has all the files....

A thought struck me, and I bit my lip, almost afraid to hope. "My brother's been missing for so long, can you look him up, see if he's in there?"

His face fell.

"Love," he brushed my hair away from my face, "I would do anything you wanted. But I'm not Quinn, or Loree, any of our tech folks. Other than my job of bringing Nixie in here, it would take me hours to find that record. Trust me. Hell, trust Nixie. If there's a trace of him in there, she'll find it as soon as we're back in contact with the team. I'll make sure it's a priority."

I nodded, chest tight. For just a moment, it seemed like I was so close, so close to finding what happened to him.

The idea of coming home to Talley and, better yet, giving her father back, glimmered before me, but it was just that.

A shiny dream.

"Sure," I said, hating my voice for sounding so small, defeated.

"Hey," he tilted my chin up till I met his eyes. "I promise."

I could believe him. I had to.

"Now, let's focus on getting out of here before

whatever little civil war Brayden's men have going on makes our lives complicated."

I couldn't help but laugh. "You mean they're not complicated now?"

"Well, maybe." He took my hand, squeezed. "Come on, I'll bet you I can boost that shuttle, if nothing else."

Those words were like music to my ears.

I wanted to get out of here so badly. And, since his mission was accomplished, there was no reason for us to stick around.

If anything, the deaths of Horg and Durl would give us the perfect excuse to leave.

Lorcan could claim fear for his own safety to leave without raising too many questions.

I was worried about Nika and all of the other women on the assembly line, but Lorcan's team would start working. They'd get everyone out, he seemed so sure of it.

He took my hand in his and led me back toward the hidden doorway. I leaned against him as we walked, letting his protective aura wash over me.

Now that he'd finished his job, I could see the end in sight, could see Talley's smiling face in my mind, waiting for me to come back to her.

We'd just crossed back into the outer office when the door to the hall slid open.

Lorcan and I froze, his hand tightening around

mine as we stared, wide-eyed, as people filed into the room.

Brayden lead the way, followed by a dozen guards, all armed to the teeth.

Lorcan let out a low growl as he stared at them.

I could feel the rage emanating from him, even as my throat went dry.

He looked ready to fight them all.

How were we supposed to get out of here now?

LORCAN

The moment I locked eyes with Brayden, I knew there wouldn't be any talking my way out of this.

He'd come here having already made up his mind.

If I wanted to get off this rock alive, then I was going to have to fight my way off it.

If I'd been alone, I could've done that easily.

But with Cintha by my side, I had to think through my actions.

Control.

Calculation.

There was probably another door leading to a secret passageway back in the server room. But what were the chances of us being able find it before they shot us?

Slim to none.

Which meant the only way out of here would be through the door they'd all just come in.

Good. I was more than ready for a fight.

With a low growl, I released Cintha's hand, pushed her back to the smaller room for protection, and readied myself.

I launched myself towards them, jumping over the desk with ease.

The guards opened fire, and I laughed, letting the joy of battle fill my veins as I twisted past the first few bolts, the lasers scorching the permasteel walls.

Smoke and the sound of crackling electronics filled the small room as I tossed the first of the guards against the wall.

Without waiting to watch him slide down into a crumpled heap, I turned to strike at the next.

That one caught my shoulder with three bolts before I reached him.

A good try, but not enough.

Grabbing his blaster, I struck him with it, knocking him sideways, out of my way.

As I moved on to the next, a small frightened whimper from Cintha reached my ears, and I spun.

"That's enough, don't you think?" Teldra held a blaster pressed against Cintha's neck.

Dammit. There *had* been another passage into the secured room. Instead of sending Cintha out of danger, I'd delivered her straight into our enemy's hands.

A snarl tore through me.

"I think you should stay still." Teldra's face was impassive, appraising.

"Don't listen to her," Cintha hissed, fury flaring her nostrils. "I'll be fine."

I could hear reinforcements arriving behind me, surrounding Brayden.

I took a step towards them, then another.

Cintha squeaked as the sister pressed the barrel harder against her tender skin, and I froze.

"I'm sorry," she whispered. "I don't know where she came from, I wasn't watching."

I'd failed her.

My brothers would be here soon, but it wouldn't be fast enough to save her from whatever Brayden and Teldra dreamed up.

The bitter thought twisted in my gut.

Shuffling behind me, Brayden appeared in my peripheral vision.

"I don't know what you thought you were doing," he spat. "Probably trying to take everything for yourself. But Horg and Durl were loyal to me, they wouldn't play your games."

What?

I shook my head. At least he still had no clue as to

what was really going on. Having disabled us, maybe he'd relax, think the threat was over.

Fine, I could play with the idiot for a while longer.

"You got me," I shrugged. "I just wanted to have a look at your files, see if what you were telling me was the truth. Can't trust a man without seeing all the numbers, you know? But that?" I pointed over to where Horgan's body still lay by the hidden door. "That wasn't me. You've got something else going on. Might want to look into that."

"What were you doing in there?" Brayden demanded.

"Gotta say, I'm pretty impressed with your computer security." I shifted my weight, watching the barrel of Teldra's blaster as I chattered on. A little lower, a little further away from Cintha.

"It'd take more of a computer jockey than I am to break through it. That's good to know. You've invested in some quality work there, I hope you know that and paid whoever did the work well." A tiny shift more, tensing and relaxing my leg muscles, biding my time. "Or did you put up the firewalls yourself? Good job."

"You were in here far too long to realize you couldn't get into the files," Brayden insisted. "What were you doing?"

I scrubbed my hair, tried to look bashful. "The girl

and I were kind of busy for a while. She had other thoughts, and well, I needed to show her otherwise."

A flash of fury crossed Teldra's face.

Why?

"So really, now that we've got all this out of the way, maybe we should--"

Screw it. He was within reach now, and I just couldn't blather on any more.

Spinning, I leapt, tackling the windbag, hands wrapped around his throat. The impact knocked his blaster from his hand as we crashed down.

"Back off," I roared at the guards. "I can pull his head off before you can find the trigger."

Brayden's face reddened, eyes rolling, hands and feet pounding the floor as he fought for air.

The job was done. It didn't matter what I did to this asshole. All the insults against every human he'd sold, every flinch from Cintha at the looks those beasts had given her, all of it could be repaid now.

"No!"

Cintha screamed behind me as a long, sustained laser blast hit the center of my back. My limbs began to go numb, but I refused to let go.

There was no other way out for us.

The dead feeling spread, my vision slowly blanking.

As I slumped back to my heels, Cintha raced across the room to me, tears streaming down her face.

And then the laser caught her, as well.

LIGHT BURNED INTO MY EYES, bright enough to be seen through my closed eyelids. I groaned and shifted, trying to figure out what the hell was going on.

"L...Lorcan, is that you?"

I let out another groan, forcing my eyes open. The light grew even brighter, and I recoiled, squeezing them shut again.

Then I took a couple deep breaths, focusing myself, and slowly opened my eyes. This time, it was bright, but the light no longer blinded me.

I looked around, trying to figure out what was going on, where I was. Had the rest of the team come and rescued me?

But when I was finally able to focus, I knew I wasn't on one of their ships or even still in Brayden's security office.

This was...different.

A forest of some sort, with bright green trees all around me. It was most definitely not the asteroid Brayden had been using for his base of operations.

Had he dropped us on some nearby planet, left us for dead?

Then I looked over and saw Cintha sitting next to me, propped up against a tree.

She was looking around, a dazed expression on her face. But that wasn't the strangest thing.

She was dressed in, hell, I couldn't have told you. Doc might have known, or Nadira.

Something long and silky, not the torn shirt I'd given her.

Like something from a painting, or fantasy vids.

What in the Void was going on here?

Dumping us on the nearest planet I could see. It made sense to want our bodies as far away from their complex as possible, especially if there was a chance people would come looking for us.

By why would they dress Cintha like that?

Then, I looked down at my own clothes and grew even more confused. I wasn't wearing the pants that were all that had remained of my outfit.

Instead, I was clad in some kind of leather armor, like something straight out of a medieval history book.

Swords and all.

At least, that was a plus.

"What is going on?" I asked, my brain struggling to piece together the puzzle.

Cintha shook her head, looking just as confused as I felt. "I have no idea. Last thing I remember was you getting shot in Brayden's office. Next thing I know, I'm here, wearing this." She waved at the silks. "How did we get here? And why are we here? And where is here?"

"I wish I knew," I said, keeping my voice low.

Void, I really wished I had some kind of idea about what was going on here.

I stood up, wobbling a little as I did so. I could feel aches and pains, but they were oddly dulled.

More items for the list of weirdness.

What was worse, when I touched the tree I'd been leaning against, it felt off, like it wasn't really a tree.

Before I could open my mouth to say something to Cintha, though, something flashed in front of my eyes.

Some kind of overlay was atop my vision. I blinked a few times, but even with my eyes closed the words were there. "New Quest! Visit the Tavern for Details!" it said in bright, flashing red.

There was a little arrow indicator, and when I moved, so did the arrow, constantly pointing in the same direction.

"Cintha...." I said, but before I could finish, she interrupted me.

"Yeah, I see it, too. What the hell is it?" She closed her eyes and started rubbing them. Then, frustrated, she threw her hands up in defeat. "What is going on here?!"

Since I didn't have any answers, I kept quiet for the

moment. An override of some kind of optics implant made the most sense.

I'd seen them on previous missions before, but we'd never used them ourselves. Doc laughed, said they were far too easy to hack.

If we needed information shown to us, we just hadn't bothered to learn the mission parameters well enough, she'd scolded.

Why would I have one now?

And why should Cintha have one, as well?

More and more questions continued to pile up, without any answers.

It was really frustrating, standing here in the middle of a forest with no idea what was going on.

But it wasn't like answers were just going to fall out of the sky if we stood there waiting for them. The only way we were going to figure out what was going on was if we went out and found the answers ourselves.

And sometimes, that meant following along with whatever crazy-ass thing was happening, and keeping alert.

Something, anything would give us a hint.

"I'm figuring this little directional arrow is telling us the way to this tavern," I muttered, thinking aloud. I figured Cintha would've come to the same conclusion, but talking helped keep my mind occupied. "We should head that way, see if we can find some other people, get some answers."

Cintha let out a sigh, then nodded. She didn't look any more pleased about that option than I felt, but it wasn't like we had many choices. She squared her shoulders as she looked at me, though, looking ready to get it over with if nothing else. "Let's go, then."

I smiled at her, hoping it would help put her at ease. But considering the shaky smile she gave me in return, it didn't seem to help much at all. Not that I could blame her. After everything that had happened in Brayden's security office, I wasn't all that sure of anything anymore.

Void, I still wasn't completely recovered from it all. I wasn't quite sure what had happened to us after that or how long I'd been out, but my body still felt off.

Had I really taken that much damage? I clearly remembered each and every lase-bolt that hit me, the searing pain that had shot through my body after each one.

Even under the best circumstances, it was going to take a while to completely heal up. Maybe I'd slept long enough to make a difference.

As I looked down at myself, there weren't any visible wounds, no signs at all of the fight. But something was still wrong.

Very wrong.

I stumbled a few times as we walked, my body shifting suddenly, my balance thrown. It was like all of my senses were out of whack, disconnected from the rest of me.

The more we walked, the worse it got. Something was very, very wrong with my body. I needed to get out of here soon, get back to Doc, and have her figure out what was wrong.

Had the lase-bolts somehow affected me more than they should have?

One thing was for sure -- it just got a hell of a lot harder to keep Cintha safe.

CINTHA

Lorcan stumbled again as we headed through the strange forest, and I moved to walk alongside him, helping brace him.

How many shots had he taken?

Vaguely I could remember hearing him roaring, threatening to kill all of them. I remembered Brayden's terrified screams as he ordered his guards to keep shooting.

I remembered the sickening sound of lase-bolt after bolt hitting Lorcan's back.

But it was all distant, hazy.

Remote.

And then, all I remembered was darkness.

I couldn't imagine what had happened after that,

how badly injured Lorcan must've been. He looked fine now, but the way he acted, he most definitely wasn't.

Even though it looked like he'd completely healed up, there was no way he could've healed that quickly, not after taking that many direct hits. Even if we'd been out for a couple days for them to transport us here, wherever here was, that still wasn't enough time to recover.

So why weren't there any signs of his wounds?

And to top it off, there was something wrong with me, too.

Every once in a while, my vision seemed to flicker.

I rubbed my eyes. Maybe something had happened to me that I didn't remember, maybe I'd been hit on the head.

My hand fisted in the fabric of my ridiculous skirt.

I couldn't afford to have anything affect my vision. The ability to see fine detail was as much a part of my livelihood as the ability to draw out the designs of my imagination.

But still, something was wrong.

One moment I'd be looking at the lush green forest, straight out of a textbook of what a green world should be like.

The next, there'd be a flash of something gray, the image gone before I could figure out what I was looking at.

It was starting to freak me out. I kept rubbing my eyes, blinking, every trick I'd learned through long nights pressing to finish a client order on deadline.

But it didn't help with the flickering any more than it made the little visual overlay go away.

When I saw Brayden again, I was going to strangle him myself, I vowed.

I hadn't a clue what he'd done to me, but whatever it was, I didn't like it.

Lorcan would give me a turn, if I asked nicely.

If there was anything left of that bastard.

"Are you sure you're okay?" I asked when we paused again for him to catch his balance.

It seemed like he really needed a doctor, but I wasn't sure where we'd find one out here in the middle of nowhere.

Our best bet probably was the tavern the stupid display kept pointing us to, assuming he could make it that far. Maybe I should leave him here and go ahead?

Yeah, because you're in perfect shape with your screwed-up vision, my inner voice said, full of sarcasm.

But Lorcan nodded, his lips pursed tight. "I'm fine. Just need some time to adjust, I guess. It's like my senses are all over the place. Like, I can see the forest, but the rest of my senses are telling me it's not there. It's weird. I think maybe I hit my head when I went down."

I nodded, pursing my lips. That didn't sound good.

Void, were we going to be able to get off this rock with both of us in bad shape?

"What about your eyes? Any trouble with that?" I asked, wondering if he was having the same flashes I was.

But he shook his head. Then he looked up at me, his eyes full of concern. "What about you? Are you okay?"

"Yeah, mostly." I said, nodding. When he kept watching me, I let out a sigh and shook my head. "Something's up with my vision. Every once in a while, I get this flickering sensation. For a brief moment, everything's gray, almost like stone. But before I can really focus on it, it's gone, and the forest is back again."

Lorcan frowned as he watched me. I could see the gears turning inside his head as he tried to figure out what was going on. "I think we need to hurry up and get to this tavern, find some other people, compare notes. See if we can figure out what is going on."

So, we continued on, this time at a slightly quicker pace. Lorcan's eyes kept darting back and forth as we walked, as if he was on high alert, keeping a lookout for any potential signs of danger.

Which, I guess, made sense, since we were in the middle of a forest without any idea where we really were.

Still, I had a feeling he wasn't telling me something. Was his pain worse than he was letting on?

It took far too long for us to reach the edge of the forest, at least in my opinion.

I had no idea how long we'd been walking, but it seemed like ages. Seriously, whoever made this little arrow thing couldn't be bothered with a chrono?

The forest opened to an old village, looking like it came right out of the past. Did villages like this actually exist in the Empire?

"Where in the Void did they take us?" I wondered.

Lorcan scanned the area, eyes narrowed. "I don't know. I've never even heard of someplace like this."

We paused, but really, there wasn't a choice.

We needed answers, and standing around wasn't going to do a thing.

The tavern bustled with people when we arrived. For a moment, I just stood there near the doorway, staring slack-jawed at the people assembled there.

All of them were dressed in strange outfits. Some were like us, in silk robes or leather armor.

Others were in full suits of metal armor, looking like the knights of old. One guy was even in a red and black full-body suit that even covered his face, two swords strapped to his back.

Now I was even more confused than ever.

But as I studied them, my vision flashed.

For a moment, the tavern was gone.

Instead, everyone was in a cave, their armor and fancy outfits gone, all of them worn and beaten down, injuries visible.

I stumbled when my vision came back to me, my head splitting.

"Are you okay?" Lorcan asked as he caught my arm, steadying me.

I shook my head, frowning. "Something's wrong here, I can feel it. Sometimes, it's like I'm seeing the way things really are, but then they're gone and I'm left wondering if I really saw it."

Lorcan nodded. "The sound in here echoes slightly, not the way a wooden tavern should sound. There're no smells of a bar, modern or not, either. I feel like I should be smelling ale and food, but all I'm getting is mold and mildew, like we're somewhere damp."

It was like a weight lifted off me.

If he thought it was wrong, even if he couldn't see what I was seeing, then I wasn't going crazy.

Right?

But if it wasn't real, then what was going on? Where were we, really?

"Let's try talking to some of the people here. See if any of them have some idea of where we are or what's going on," Lorcan suggested.

Already, his eyes were scanning the room, looking

over the people. He had the look of someone who'd done things like this before, and I wished I knew more about him, more about his past.

How did he get this kind of mission in the first place? But this wasn't the time to start questioning him. There'd be plenty of time for that once we got somewhere safe.

"Yeah, okay," I said, though suddenly I wasn't thrilled about going up and talking to these people. For all I knew, they worked for Brayden.

Had an arrangement to take care of whoever he dropped off this way.

Maybe this was just another stop in his human pipeline, just a very, very different kind of clientele.

But I didn't get any vibes of aggression, no threats as people checked us out.

Just oddness.

A handful of people chatted nearby. All of them looked happy and friendly, so I decided to head over there first. They all stopped talking the moment I approached.

I wanted to turn back around, to run back over to Lorcan, but I forced myself to keep walking.

I could do this, I told myself, over and over again.

This new me, nervous at everything, was just leftover nonsense from being kidnapped.

Okay. Maybe not total nonsense. But I wasn't going

to be held hostage to it.

"You must be a new player," a big woman said to me. She stood at the same height as Lorcan, but leaner, despite her muscles. She had on maroon armor, made entirely of metal. Sitting on the floor next to her was a giant war hammer that locked like it could've knocked down the entire tavern!

This woman wouldn't have looked out of place in the middle of one of those vid games the kids loved playing. "Haven't seen you around here before."

"We, uh, just got here," I said, not wanting to give too much information. If Brayden thought he'd left us here to die, then I didn't want anyone working for him to know we were still alive.

They all seemed to know what they were doing though, and didn't look lost like we were.

"Well, you picked a good time!" The woman said with a broad grin. Her voice was loud and boisterous, easily carrying throughout the entire tavern. "The quest should be starting soon."

"Quest?" I asked.

The woman laughed, then shook her head. "Yeah, guess if you're new here, you wouldn't know all the ins and outs yet. Every once in a while, they'll announce a bonus quest to go hunt down some enemies nearby. We get points for all the loot we gather, which gives us a chance to level up and get new equipment." She patted the war hammer next to us. "It's the best way to progress here. There's other, minor work you can do, but the quests are where the real stuff is."

I nodded, pretending I had any idea what she was talking about. It all certainly sounded like one of those vid games.

But why would these people be talking like game characters? I didn't seem to be any closer to answers than I had been when we woke up.

Before I could ask anything else though, my vision flashed again, making me stumble. My heart pounded as I looked around, my breathing coming in ragged gasps. We were all standing in a large stone cave, with very little light to illuminate the place. The large woman in front of me was no longer large, nor was she armored. She was smaller than me, short and skinny, looking like she hadn't had a decent meal in a long time. Her clothes were faded and tattered. She had bruises and cuts up and down her arms.

Then, before I could really get a look at anyone else, my vision was back to the tavern. The group stared at me, eyebrows raised, as I struggled to catch my breath. My heart continued to pound as I tried to process everything I'd seen.

"Are you okay?" The large woman asked.

I nodded, standing up straight and squaring my shoulders. I could do this, I kept repeating. After a few seconds, I'd calmed down enough to speak again. "Does your vision ever flicker in and out?" I found myself asking, needing to know if I was the only one experiencing this. "Like, everything looks normal one second, then it's all dark and gray the next?"

The people standing there looked at each other for a moment, Then, one after the other, they each shook their heads and shrugged. "Sounds like your pod might be defective," the large woman said with a shrug of her own. "You should probably contact the GMs or something. Maybe they can fix it for you."

I opened my mouth to ask what she meant when words appeared in front of my eyes again. Only this time, instead of telling me to head to the tavern, they said "Quest Start!" with a new directional arrow.

"Well, guys," the large woman said to her companions, "let's get going!" She hefted up her massive war hammer, then turned and headed toward the entrance to the tavern. The others followed her, nodding to me as they walked by.

The rest of the tavern was beginning to file out as well. I looked around for Lorcan, wanting to find out what he'd learned so we could figure out our next course of action. He shouldn't have been hard to spot, since normally he stood well above everyone else. But half the people in here seemed to be his height or taller, which was crazy.

The only people with his size and build I'd ever seen in my life were his brothers when they were on patrol.

So, how could there be so many large, muscular-looking people in this place?

Then I spotted him. Except, it wasn't Lorcan my eyes fell upon.

Daix.

He was standing near the back of the tavern, wearing leather armor like Lorcan, a sword and dagger attached to his belt.

But even he seemed bigger, stronger, healthier than he'd been in years.

My heart had been pounding earlier, but now it seemed to have completely stopped.

All I could do was stand there and stare, waiting for him to disappear like the flashes did.

But he stayed there, leaning against the wall, looking like he was waiting for everyone else to leave before making his move.

My legs went on autopilot, walking slowly at first, then running, pushing people out of my way.

If this was my mind playing tricks on me, I needed to know.

If it wasn't...

I had to get to him before he disappeared, I just had to.

LORCAN

oid, I need to get out of here.

Something was definitely going on.

I've been in plenty of taverns and bars, wooden buildings, weird places.

All sizes, some busy, some empty. I know how footsteps should sound in one, how voices should echo.

Wherever we were, it was wrong.

The footsteps were too hard, the voices too echoey. It was like we were in a small confined space, with hard floors and walls.

My eyes told me the place was made entirely out of wood, but if I closed my eyes and just focused on my ears, it sounded more like stone.

I had to focus to hear it, though, otherwise it was

like the sounds of wood and stone mingling together inside my head.

What was going on here?

I'd drifted around the room, picking up bits and pieces of the conversations. Everyone seemed to be talking about the quest in some way or another.

Some were talking about strategy, others about new armor or weapons they'd picked up.

Some had personal goals they wanted to achieve, others were trying to earn enough to buy something new.

No one made any mentions of anything strange going on. It was as if this was all completely normal to them.

No one seemed distressed or confused, like they'd been dumped here against their will.

Apparently, Cintha and I were special.

That was never a good thing.

I spotted her near the back of the tavern, talking with another guy. She looked frustrated while he seemed to be laughing.

I headed over there to figure out what was going on.

"Come on, Daix, be serious!" Cintha practically shouted as I got closer.

Daix.

Her brother, the one she'd been looking for.

What was he doing here?

I let out a sigh as I moved to stand next to Cintha. Just another question we needed an answer to.

The list was stacking up.

"Finally found a job I'm suited for, thought that's what you wanted." He grinned at her, showing off his pristine white teeth.

I raised an eyebrow. What sort of job?

But he didn't clarify anything.

"I can't believe you're here, that's all. Never figured you to be into this kinda deal."

Cintha let out a string of curses as she glared at her brother. "I swear I'm going to throttle you if you don't give me a straight answer."

He patted Cintha on the back, still grinning like he didn't have a care in the world. "Oh, come on. You're always so serious all the time. Can't you have a little fun once in a while? After all, isn't that why you signed up? To have fun?"

"That's what I'm trying to tell you, you idiot! I didn't sign up for any of this. I don't want to be here, wherever here is!" Cintha looked ready to pull her hair out.

Daix stopped laughing, as if he were trying to process what she'd said. "You must be off your rocker. The only way to become a tester is to sign up for it or get promoted. I had to wait ages before I got chosen." He shrugged, unconcerned. "Sure, I miss Talley and you and all, but it's worth it to be able to be on the front lines of this game and send money back home. Now if you'll excuse me, I need to get started on this quest or all the good stuff will be gone."

With that, he brushed past Cintha and walked away without turning back. She stood there, fuming for a moment, her eyes staring a hole into Daix's back. Then, finally, she let out a huff. "Void, he can be such an idiot."

"Want me to go knock some sense into him?" I offered.

Daix seemed like the kind of guy who needed to have the information smacked into him once in a while before he'd learn.

But Cintha shook her head, frowning as Daix left the tavern. "No, he's not going to be much use right now. He said something about a game, though, any idea what he meant by that?"

"I heard some people talking like this was all some kind of game for them, but I'm not sure what any of them meant."

An idea lingered just at the edge of my consciousness, but I couldn't quite grasp it. What was I missing?

Before I could spend too much time considering it, a new message popped up in my visual field. "Bonus Raid! The top five players who bring back the most jewels will earn a bonus! Happy Hunting!"

The bright red letters flashed right in front of my eyes.

I let out a sigh and shook my head. It looked like we'd have to spend a bit more time following these instructions until we had more information.

"I guess we should follow the others for now, see where they lead. If nothing else, they don't seem to be in any danger."

Cintha playfully bumped me with her hip. "That'll be a nice change, at least. We're not going to get much out of exploring an empty tavern."

A flash of pain shot up my side, but quickly dulled.

I wasn't quite sure what the message meant by jewels, but I figured we'd find out soon enough if we followed everyone else.

I hoped.

Cintha nodded and the two of us followed the last of the people out of the bar. When we stepped back outside, the path we'd taken earlier seemed to be gone.

The forest seemed to have thickened while we were in there, grown closer to the tavern, the rest of the buildings of the village having disappeared.

I shook my head.

Were we leaving through a different door?

My gut tightened. There was no option except to follow the trail the other people were already heading down.

My senses seemed to scream even louder, all the warning signs of danger flashing inside my brain but without any indication of where or what the danger was.

We needed to get out of here, but I couldn't see it.

"The flashes in your vision don't happen to show another path out of here, do they?" I asked, trying not to get my hopes up.

But Cintha shook her head, peering all around, as if hoping one would magically appear, but her expression didn't brighten in the least. "All I can see is gray. It still looks like stone, if I had to guess, wherever we've been. The forest, the tavern, anywhere. And the trees don't look right, even when I see them."

When I reached out, closed my eyes and touched the bark, it felt like hard stone mixed with wood somehow, unlike any single substance I'd encountered before.

It was starting to throw my head for a loop, leaving me with a pounding headache as my brain tried to sort everything out.

It really did seem like I had wires crossed somehow.

The possibilities weren't good.

If I was deteriorating, if Doc and the rest of the pack weren't here to control me when that happened, I'd be a danger to everyone around me.

But that wouldn't explain what Cintha saw in her flashes.

If I wasn't, then what was going on?

Even the ground felt wrong to walk on. What should have been soft dirt or grass alternated between that and hardness, something that made a slight echo.

If I focused too hard, it just made splitting pain shoot through my head. A couple times, I had to stop and squeeze my eyes shut and massage my temples before we could continue on.

It didn't help that I could still feel the echoes of pain going through the rest of my body.

Pain I was used to. An old, familiar friend.

But I knew exactly how my body should be reacting. What it needed to heal. What every step of that process should feel like.

This shallow echo of it? It wasn't how it normally felt, even when I was only partly healed up. Everything about this situation just seemed to confuse me.

It was like questions stacked upon questions, without even a single answer.

"Are you sure you're going to be okay?" Cintha asked, her worry evident on her beautiful face.

I hated not being able to be a rock for her, be the one she could lean on without ever wavering.

Next time, I'd do a better job of ripping Brayden's throat out.

I smiled at her and nodded, not willing to give up,

no matter how confused I was or how screwed up my senses seemed to be.

There was no way I'd give up on my mission.

Or Cintha.

I had promised to protect her, to get her back home.

And damn it, I was going to fulfill that promise no matter what.

Control.

Calculation.

Whatever the hell was going on, I'd figure it out.

We'd figure it out.

"Yeah, I'm good," I told her, steeling my resolve. I'd been injured worse, trapped on worse planets. If nothing else, I'd keep going until the rest of the pack found me.

They'd keep her safe, finish the mission, get her home.

And that would do.

Cintha stumbled again, and I reached out to steady her.

It was sweet of her to be worried about me, but she didn't seem to be in the best shape herself. "What about you? Are you okay?"

She took a couple deep breaths, then nodded. "Yeah, I'm okay. It's just really disorienting when these flashes hit. It's like one moment I'm here, and the next, I'm somewhere else. But before I can adjust to the new place, it's gone and I'm right back where I started." She let out a breath, like she was frustrated with herself. "I wish I could hold onto the flashes, could make them stay long enough for me to study them, get an idea of where we really are. Because, no matter what this place seems to be, I know something's going on."

I nodded, agreeing with her assessment. I may not be having the same flashes as her, my eyes being the one thing that seemed to be staying focused, but the rest of my senses couldn't say the same thing.

Which was going to make things a lot harder, if things went sideways. Which, in my experience, they always did at some point.

Without much alternative, we kept walking forward, heading through the dense forest or wherever it was we actually were.

We didn't have to walk much longer before the sounds of a fight echoed toward us.

Metal clashing against metal, screams and grunts, filled the air, coming from a clearing ahead of us. The two of us exchanged a look, then took deep breaths and walked into the clearing.

CINTHA

Everyone from the tavern was engaged in battle; the clearing was filled to the brim with all sorts of creatures.

Orcs and kobolds and trolls. None of them real.

But all of them here.

My heart pounded as I watched these people hack apart the creatures, laughing as much as they were shouting.

Even Daix was hacking his way through them with his sword. Daix had never really been a gentle guy, but he also hadn't been overly violent, either.

He wasn't the kind of guy to just slaughter creature after creature without the slightest bit of remorse.

And a sword? When the hell had he ever learned to use such a thing?

Each time someone would kill one of the creatures, they'd kneel down and retrieve something off the body.

It took me a few moments to realize it was some sort of crystal or jewel, probably whatever the last message had referred to.

My brain was so overloaded with everything going on that all I could do was stand there and stare.

When I glanced over at Lorcan, his eyes darted from person to person, creature to creature, his right hand gripping the hilt of his sword.

His knuckles had gone white from how tightly he gripped it, and he looked torn between wading into the battle and turning back the way we came.

"What is going on?" I found myself asking, trying to make sense of it all.

Creatures like that didn't exist in real life. Even out here, in the fringes of the Empire, there was no way those things were real. But they sure looked and sounded real as the people attacked them without mercy. I could hear their cries of anger and pain, could smell their stench even from where I stood.

"I wish I knew," Lorcan mumbled.

Then, a flash hit me. The forest and clearing were gone, leaving in its place an open cavern, barely lit.

My vision waivered, but I fought to study the fine points, forced my focus to be on what was in front of me, every detail, just as I always had. I could do this. I *would* do this.

The people all looked like ordinary humans again. There was just enough light to study the people closest to us. Their weapons weren't swords or hammers or maces; they were all wielding what looked like pickaxes, all dressed in ragged, worn coveralls.

But the most jarring part wasn't the people, it was the creatures. They were all gone now, leaving in their place giant worms.

At least, that was the only way I could think to describe them.

Some were larger than others, somehow standing vertical. Others crawled on the ground, looking more like they were trying to escape than attack.

Those that were fighting back seemed to be spitting acid or something, though it didn't have much effect on the people.

The ones who were rearing up had small stinging tentacles that weren't much more effective than the acid spray.

One of the people next to us killed a worm and it slumped onto its side, no longer moving. The human fighter set his pickaxe down and squatted next to the worm, wrenching open it's stomach to plunge his hand inside.

Moments later, he pulled his hand back out,

wrapped around something glowing that he hurriedly stuffed into his belt pouch before picking up his pickaxe again and moving on to the next worm.

My stomach lurched as I stared at the guy, realization hitting me. The movements he'd done to open the worm's stomach and retrieve whatever he'd grabbed.

They were the same motions we'd been using on the assembly lines. They weren't having us make parts for them. They were training us for this.

"Void...." I muttered under my breath. Lorcan must've heard, though, since his arms were around me in an instant. He held me steady, letting me brace myself against his body.

Up close, I could see his clothes were just another set of overalls, cleaner than the others, but certainly not armor.

And the sword at his waist was no longer a sword, but a pickaxe identical to the others.

A glance down at my own body told me I was in a matching set, gray and rough. No silken dress, no jewels.

"What do you see?" Lorcan asked, his mouth right next to my ear. Even now, his hot breath right against my skin made me tingle.

"Everything's all wrong," I said at last, taking a deep breath before telling him what I saw. The flash lasted longer this time, and it wasn't until I was halfway through telling him what I'd seen that I lost my focus, the fantasy images returning.

It was somehow more jarring this time, like something had been ripped away from me.

Whatever was going on here, it wasn't good.

I wasn't sure how I knew, but the cavern images definitely seemed to be the real deal, more so than these fantasy creatures and weapons.

"It sounds like whatever implant is giving us those visual overlays is completely overriding our senses." Lorcan let out a growl of frustration. "Which is completely illegal." He let out a bark of laughter. "Not that I'm in any position to argue."

His body tensed against mine. He was getting angrier the longer we were trapped here, and I couldn't blame him.

But now we had an idea of what was going on.

We just needed to figure out some way to stop it.

"Should we just head back to the tavern place? See if I can find another way out?" I asked, wondering if that would be a better idea than sticking around here.

Despite how the orcs and all seemed to be behaving, the worms I'd seen didn't seem to be all that aggressive. They looked more like they were just defending themselves, trying to get away from the people slaughtering them.

But just because they weren't really attacking right now, didn't mean they wouldn't later. If they realized the people weren't going to stop, they might decide to take things to the next level and see just how many people they can kill.

One of the guys let out a scream as he crumpled to the ground in front of what looked like an orc. He stopped moving, then his body disappeared altogether.

The people around him laughed, like it was no big deal. "He's gonna be pissed when he wakes up in his pod! He'll have lost a ton of points."

None of them so much as batted an eye at their comrade when he'd died. Tears welled up inside me, knowing what I'd just seen was most likely real, that the guy really was dead.

It wasn't just some game, with them back in pods or wherever they thought they were. This was all real, with just some shiny overlay masking the horror of what was going on.

Void, how many people had already died in these caverns? How many more would die before we were able to figure a way out of here?

Before Lorcan could respond, though, he stood up straighter, every muscle in his body tensing at once. "Something's coming," he announced.

He didn't stop scanning around us, even though he knew his eyes couldn't be trusted. "Do you see

TAKEN   195

anything? Something different than the regular creatures they're fighting?"

I tried to force the change, but my vision was still showing me the fantasy creatures, rather than reality. None of them appeared any different, nor did I see any new ones appearing.

What could have his triggered senses?

I wasn't even sure why he could still hear and smell parts of reality, but I figured it was just another glitch, the same way I could occasionally see glimpses of what was really there.

Then, as the creatures started to roar, Lorcan clasped his hands over his ears, doubling over in pain. The sound was loud, but it wasn't ear-piercing or anything.

I couldn't figure out why he'd be so affected by that but not any of the other sounds of the battle going on. Was it part of the glitches? Was it maybe amplifying the sound for him?

"We need to get out of here," Lorcan said through gritted teeth. "Whatever's coming, it's not good. Void, their screeching feels like it's going to split my head in half!"

"Screeching?" I asked, confused. I didn't hear any screeching, just the dull roars of the fantasy creatures.

Then, it hit me. He must've been hearing the worms,

not the orcs and trolls and whatever nonsense the implants were feeding us.

He could hear what they actually sounded like, whereas I could only see them.

No one else responded at all.

Lorcan nodded, his hands clasped to his ears. "I think whatever they're fighting, they've called for help."

A lump formed in my throat. No matter how many times I tried to swallow it, it just wouldn't go away.

Lorcan was always so assured.

When Brayden was shooting at us or when we woke up in the middle of a strange forest, he'd kept his composure.

So, if whatever was coming had him nervous, then we needed to get going. Needed to get as far away from here as we possibly could.

Then, the trees at the far side of the clearing split apart as a massive creature barreled through them, roaring louder than the others, its voice drowning out all the other sounds.

Lorcan dropped to his knees and let out his own cries of pain. His hands were still clamped over his ears, his eyes were squeezed shut, as he tried to muffle the sound.

Void, I'd never seen anything like it.

It stood at least three times as high as the tallest of

the orcs, moving on four legs, with multiple long necks attached to its body.

How was anyone supposed to fight a creature like that, I wondered as I stared helplessly up at it.

Did these people fight creatures like that all the time? Was this just another day in their lives?

I gripped the dagger at my belt, heart thundering. My instincts shrieked at me to get away, to run, but I refused to just leave Lorcan there.

I stood my ground, watching as the other people turned to face the creature. A few grinned and approached it, gripping their weapons tightly.

The creature lashed out with its tail and batted three of them aside like they were made of paper. I watched in horror as their bodies slammed against the wall of trees, knowing they'd just hit a stone wall.

The ones that hadn't gotten hit stared at their companions, then started backing away, their weapons shaking.

Interesting.

This wasn't something they were used to fighting.

Which meant we really, really needed to get out of there.

I bent down to help Lorcan as the players closest to us started backing out of the clearing, heading toward the tavern.

As the creature started to push its way deeper into

the clearing, people began to run, terror visible on their faces as they ran past us.

Lorcan managed to stand on shaky legs, glaring up at the creature. "I don't think they're going to be able to outrun it," he said with a grim, determined look on his face. "We need to stop it, here and now."

LORCAN

I gritted my teeth as I pulled the pickaxe off my belt. It looked like a sword, but Cintha had assured me it wasn't, and as I tested its weight and balance, I knew she was right.

Anyone with some actual weapons training would know right off the bat that this wasn't how a sword felt in your hands.

But then, judging from what I'd seen of the fighting, none of the people here had any combat experience.

They were all just swinging and hacking at anything that got within reach.

Which was the reason they'd gotten swept aside like garbage before running away. The idiots thought they could actually escape that thing.

No, the moment it laid eyes on us, it'd chosen us as

its targets. Even if it had to pursue us for the rest of its life, there was no way that creature would let even a single person live.

It had come running when the smaller worms had called for it, which meant it was protecting them. If I had to guess, I'd say it was the mother worm, some alien animal species I'd never heard of, or wanted to.

And all these people had just slaughtered its babies.

No way would she forget that.

But as much as I assumed it was another, much more massive worm, it was hard to make that mesh with the image in front of me.

It looked like a hydra, with multiple snapping heads that could easily swallow me whole. Without being able to trust my vision, and without a good weapon, this fight was going to be nearly impossible to win.

But damn if I was going to just roll over and accept defeat.

Not exactly built that way, were we?

Soon, all that were left in the clearing was Cintha and me and the creatures. The orcs had all scattered as the hydra moved forward.

Though they all looked mean and angry, the way they moved told me they were scared, hiding behind this larger creature for protection.

Just another lie, thanks to the damned visual

implants or whatever they'd done to us while we'd been unconscious.

"Are you sure about this?" Cintha asked as I stepped forward.

I nodded.

Alright.

Maybe not exactly sure.

But I wasn't going to let her know that. As long as I stayed calm, she would stay calm. And if I wanted to have any chance of beating this creature, then I needed to have her there by my side.

I couldn't trust my vision, but I could trust hers.

Since I had no idea which heads would be real, I'd need to hope she could see through the illusion soon and guide me.

Other than that, I'd just have to focus on evading the creature until I could get some hits in.

When I was halfway across the clearing, the beast lashed out with its tail, trying to swipe me aside like it had the others.

It took all my strength to jump up and over it, landing in a crouch and readying myself for the next attack. Judging by the way the wind had hit me from the creature's movement, it's tail, or whatever it really was, was massive and would easily knock me aside if I wasn't careful.

"Let me know if you see a weak spot!" I shouted to Cintha.

If Cintha replied, I didn't hear it.

The hydra lashed forward with one of its heads, and I barely had time to roll out of the way. Dirt flew up from where the head had impacted the ground, but it was small pebbles I felt peppering my skin in the aftermath. It also told me just how strong the creature was if it was able to break the stone that easily.

"How am I supposed to beat this thing?" I grumbled under my breath.

The beast lashed forward with two of its heads this time, seeming like it was trying to cut off my escape. I jumped this time, though, instead of rolling and swung out with the pickaxe, but it seemed to just go right through the creature without touching it.

Which meant the head I'd tried to strike was just another illusion.

Fine.

I darted in and swung the pickaxe at the creature's stomach and felt the metal sink into it. But when I tried to pull it back, the pickaxe was stuck firm in the creature's tough skin.

I could've wrenched it free, if the creature hadn't lashed forward with one of its heads again, forcing me to dodge backward, the impact jarring through me.

I took deep breaths as I studied the creature,

hoping to find a weakness, but without being able to trust my eyes, I was literally going into this fight blind.

Blind.

I ripped a piece of my shirt off, then tied it around my head, blocking my vision completely. If I couldn't trust my vision, then I needed to be able to ignore it.

Whoever had designed this system, hadn't counted on a player with heightened senses crashing their little game.

Without the distraction of my eyes, I should be able to focus on what was left. My augmented senses of smell and hearing were too strong for the implant to completely override. With my sight cut off, they became even stronger.

"Watch out!" Cintha shouted just as I felt the air around me move.

I jumped backward barely in time for the creature to strike the ground in front of me.

I dodged a few more strikes, then stumbled over something, falling backward and scarcely avoiding another strike. My heart skipped a few dozen beats as I reached around to see what I'd fallen over, then I cursed when I realized what it was.

Just as I'd thought, the guy who'd died hadn't just vanished, going back to some pod or whatever like the others had said. They were all really here, fighting these creatures while thinking they're nice and safe somewhere else.

Which was why they'd all been so reckless, laughing and joking as they attacked these creatures with no real skill or finesse. They weren't fighting for their lives or being forced into this. They were going out here of their own free will, just because they thought it was all a game.

So, this was the system Brayden had really been setting up, why he'd been so proud of what he'd built.

He wasn't just kidnapping people for slave labor, training them for what clients demanded.

He'd created a way to have slaves eagerly complete the tasks assigned to them. It didn't matter how terrifying or dangerous the jobs were, they'd charge in and get it done, just because they thought they were all safe and sound somewhere else.

Like the women at the dinner party.

Or the fighters afterwards.

Void, how had I not seen this sooner?

"Lorcan, watch out!" Cintha yelled, bringing me back to the here and now.

My body tensed, and I reached around until I found the handle of the fallen guy's pickaxe. Rolling out of the way, I managed to avoid the brunt of the creature's attack.

Stone pelted my body as dull aches started to make

themselves known in various spots. Then the pain vanished, leaving nothing but a dull echo.

I frowned as I continued backing away from the creature. The implant must've been blocking my pain receptors somehow, convincing my brain I was perfectly fine, even when I wasn't.

Clever.

It was a good way to keep slaves working, even when their bodies should've been about ready to drop. It would eventually kill the workers, but anyone employing this system wouldn't care.

They were disposable.

Anger welled up inside me and I tightened my grip on the pickaxe, determined to put an end to this creature so we could get out of here and shut down this whole system.

"Cintha!" I shouted as I braced myself. "I need you to tell me when it's about to strike with its head!"

Cintha shouted in acknowledgement, her voice echoing around me.

I braced myself, taking deep breaths and trying to push my senses to their limit.

If I got back, *when* I got back, Doc would be thrilled to know about how far her enhancements could be stretched.

Hell. She'd probably be excited about the entire crazy set up.

Maybe I could find someone else to take the implant out that wouldn't just find a way to make it better.

Surely we knew someone that wasn't a mad scientist, right?

"It's coming!" Cintha shouted, and I focused on the vibrations in the air, the change in the scents, everything.

I waited until the very last moment before jumping up and forward. As gravity started pulling me back down, I swung the pickaxe, burying it in the creature's head.

It screeched, the sound feeling like it was turning my brain to mush, but I refused to let go, refused to give it a chance to regroup.

I adjusted my grip with my left hand, then used my right to probe its hard skin, looking for a weak spot. A finger sank into a slightly softer spot.

Maybe an eye?

I didn't bother to ask Cintha, just fixed in my mind's eye where it was in relation to the pickaxe I still clung to and scrambled for the dagger at my belt.

Jamming it as hard as I could into the soft spot, the screeching intensified. I felt like my brain was splitting in half, but I still couldn't quit.

I pulled the knife out, then stabbed it in again and again.

The creature started thrashing around even harder

now, and I had to struggle to keep my grip on the pickaxe as it fought to throw me off.

I took a deep breath, then pulled the knife back out and felt around some more, looking for another week spot. If the first one had really been its eye, there should be another right about...

Aha! I found it!

Before it could dislodge me, I stabbed it in its other eye, pushing the knife as deep into the creature as I possibly could. It reared up, nearly dumping me down its back, and let out another head-splitting scream of pain.

Before I could fall backward, the creature slammed to the ground, the sheer force of it sending me bouncing off.

"Lorcan!" Cintha yelled.

Her voice sounded distant, and I fought to sit up, brace for another attack.

But nothing moved, no tremor through the ground, no vibration.

We were all that still lived in the cavern.

I hoped.

CINTHA

Despite my struggle to keep focused on reality, my vision flipped back to the game overlay just in time to see the hydra slump to the ground.

Its head hit with enough force to shake the entire area and send Lorcan flying away from it. I winced as I watched him tumble end over end until he finally came to a stop.

His avatar looked perfectly fine, but I knew there was no way he'd survived something like that without a scratch.

"Lorcan!" I shouted as my legs began to move on their own. Quicker than I've ever moved, I was by Lorcan's side, kneeling down next to him.

He tried to sit up, and when I moved to help him, I felt blood coming from his side. Lorcan let out a groan but didn't seem to be in nearly as much pain as he should've been, judging by how much blood I could feel seeping between my fingers.

Was that another "feature" of this stupid game? To mask pain so the people involved wouldn't realize they were hurt?

"Can you hear me?" I asked, wondering just how badly hurt he was.

Thankfully, he nodded as he sat up, pulling the blindfold off.

He had to blink a few times, like he was trying to clear his head, but otherwise it seemed like he was fully conscious, at least. Be thankful for small favors, right?

"You should probably rest here for a bit. It feels like you have quite a few injuries from that fight." I really wasn't keen on just hanging out in this clearing, cave, whatever it was.

All the smaller monsters seemed to have vanished during the battle, but they could come back at any time. And if they came back, Lorcan wasn't in any condition to fight them off.

I certainly wouldn't be any use in a fight.

Lorcan shook his head, though, clearly not liking that plan any more than I did.

He tried to stand, wobbled, but caught himself, a muscle at the edge of his jaw jumping.

"Easy, Lorcan, easy." I held him tightly, not wanting him to fall and hurt himself even more.

As much as I wanted to get out of there, I didn't need Lorcan bleeding out, either. "You're bleeding. I can feel it. We need to find a way to stop the bleeding before we go anywhere."

Lorcan shook his head, even though he was gritting his teeth. "We need to go, need to get out of here." Lorcan tried to pull away from me, but considering I was able to keep my grip on him fairly easily, I knew he wasn't in any shape to be going anywhere.

"Not until we stop that bleeding, at least. I don't need you passing out from blood loss." I helped him move over to where the wall of the cavern was, though it still looked like an overgrown forest.

He didn't fight me too hard, even when I forced him to sit back down. "So, did all your super-spy training teach you how to bandage a wound? Because, I have to say, working with jewelry didn't teach me how to treat much more than some burns."

Lorcan let out a chuckle, then started removing what looked like his leather armor, but I knew was just the top of his overalls.

He reached inside to feel around. He let out a hiss, presumably when he found the source of all the bleeding, then let out a sigh.

"I'm going to need to rest for a while," he frowned. "This isn't ideal."

"Want to tell me what about this is?" I teased, wishing I could help, wishing we were anywhere other than here.

"Come here." Gently, I tugged him until he lay with his head in my lap. Running my hand through his hair, I thought about all the times I'd soothed Talley. The years where she needed a nap, but had no intention of going down for one.

I smothered a giggle.

Even wounded, I was pretty sure that Lorcan didn't want to be compared to a fussy toddler.

"Just rest, honey," I murmured. "I'll keep an eye out, try to keep practicing, figuring out how I'm seeing past their illusion."

"Tell me more about your shop," he answered hazily. "It's always feels so tiny when I go in, I'm scared I'm going to break something."

I snorted. "I doubt it. You're the most graceful man I've ever seen in my life."

"Not introducing you to my brothers," he rambled on. "Not safe, you know."

"I've met some of them, remember?" I shook my head. "And my best friend is married to one? I think they're safe enough."

"Hrumph."

And that was the last of his conversation.

I shifted until my back was against what I knew was the cavern wall, fingers absently stroking through his hair while I tried to figure out what caused the implant to switch.

The clearing was perfect around us, trees gently moving in the breeze, grass deep green, small flowers scattered throughout.

That was odd.

The flowers seemed to repeat. Pink, pink, then a blue one. All the same, but different colored blooms.

Three long tufts of grass, then another batch of flowers, arranged just the same.

The instant I saw it, my vision shifted. The cavern, the poor dead game player, the mutilated bodies of whatever those worm creatures were, all gone, replaced by a clear-domed light shining weakly from the center of the cavern roof.

And then a blink, and it was back to the shady clearing.

I studied the forest, looking for flaws. There. The swirling pattern of the thick tree directly across from us repeated two trees further along the circle. Even the twisted branches were a copy.

Back to the cavern again. While from the clearing, it had looked like there was a single path in and out, when

I could examine the cavern, it was clear there were multiple tunnels leading into the space.

And with every flaw I found in the overlay, it became easier to flip back to reality, hold it longer.

Apparently, they hadn't been prepared for someone to look closely.

Good.

I'd take any advantage we could get.

"We should get back to the tavern," Lorcan said after a short while. "I should be okay to walk now."

"You've got to be kidding," I argued. "It's been an hour, tops."

He pushed up from my lap slowly, as if testing muscles as he moved. "I've been better, but this will do." He reached back into his overalls, closed his eyes. "Bleeding's stopped, at least. I think we better get moving."

Lorcan stood, stretching his shoulders, flexing his legs.

He was right. Somehow, he was actually better.

And... in the grand scheme of things, it was just one more mystery. For a change, it wasn't something that was trying to kill me.

I could live with that.

"You've got so many things to explain," I grumbled as he pulled me to my feet.

He flashed that cocky grin, and my annoyance

melted. "I promise. Just not until I'm certain of where we are, alright?"

Yup. I could live with that, too.

And him.

Crap. Not going there, not now.

Luckily, all of my stray thoughts got back in line when he stumbled a few steps back down the path.

"Not quite as healed as you thought?" I hurried to his side, pulled his arm around my shoulders.

He snarled in irritation. "Stupid implant. Can't trust anything." He shot a quick look at me, squeezed me tight to him. "But you. That's an easy one."

But nothing else was easy. It took three times as long to get back to the tavern as the trip out. We didn't have a stream of people to follow this time, but the visual overlay didn't seem to want us to go anywhere else, guiding us along a winding path through a dense forest.

Along the way I practiced, looking for more flaws in the overlay. I could see tunnels branching off from where we walked, but who knew what was down there waiting for us?

At another stumble, we stopped for a while. "Maybe you need more sleep," I suggested, but he shook his head.

"If we're just in a cave somewhere, I don't think we

should be alone. There should be safety in numbers. Let's get back."

I still wasn't completely sure who Lorcan worked for, but damn if I was going to end up explaining to them that I let him die down here in these caverns.

Eventually, after a few breaks to catch our breath, the wooden facade of the tavern came into view.

I couldn't help but risk a tentative smile as I lead Lorcan inside, hoping we'd be able to sit there and rest for a bit without having to worry about creatures ambushing us, or whatever other surprises this place had for us.

And maybe someone in there would know a way out. I doubted it, since they all assumed they were safely in pods somewhere else.

But there was a chance, and if nothing else, we'd have a moment to sit and think.

There was a table and some chairs open near the back corner of the tavern, so I led Lorcan over there, helping him into one of the chairs.

Even though his avatar looked perfectly fine, I could hear his heavy breathing and had felt him shaking as I'd supported his weight while we walked. "How are you feeling?" I asked, knowing he probably wouldn't give me a straight answer.

Lorcan looked up at me and smiled. He looked perfectly happy, but I knew that was all just part of the illusion. He had to be hurt, his smile forced. "I'll survive," he said at last.

And I nodded, wondering how he could be so sure of that. Had his senses started clearing up? Did he know the extent of his injuries? Or was he just trying to put on a brave face so he wouldn't worry me?

He reached out and took my hand in his, lacing his fingers with mine.

"Trust me, Cintha. I'm tougher than I look. It'll take a while to get back to one hundred percent, but I'll live. I promise."

"Okay," I said simply.

Part of me wanted to scream that he was lying and just being brave, but the other part of me did trust him.

There just wasn't any other choice. And the longer we stayed quiet, the better his chances were.

For a while, the two of us just sat there in silence, watching the rest of the room, listening to what everyone around us was saying.

I found Daix in the center of a crowd in the far corner. For a moment, I considered fighting my way through his happy band of warrior-idiots, shaking someone until I got actual answers, but honestly, I wasn't up to dealing with him.

It was unlikely Daix knew anything if he thought that somehow playing this game was sending money home to me and Talley.

Some were bragging about how many jewels they'd managed to score from the raid. Others were lamenting about having to cut the raid short due to the hydra appearing. They discussed equipment, talking about different things they could get that would be able to slay the new challenge.

I wanted to tell them all how stupid they were being, that none of this was real and no matter what "equipment" they got, one of those "hydras" would kill them, without a doubt.

Then, a jingle sounded around the bar. Everyone froze in place and stopped talking as red letter appeared before our eyes.

This time, instead of announcing a quest or raid, the big red letters said "INVASION!".

Everyone stared around at each other, all looking confused.

Then small letters scrolled across. "An orc has invaded the tavern! The player who defeats it will receive a bonus reward!"

Everyone looked around excitedly, trying to find the supposed orc. Maybe a worm had followed us back?

Then I noticed everyone start to look our way as they stood, drawing their weapons.

My heart pounded hard enough that it should've been audible. A lump formed in my throat, refusing to go away no matter how many times I swallowed.

Slowly, as if time had slowed to a crawl, I turned to look at Lorcan.

Except, he was gone now.

He'd been replaced by the image of one of the orcs.

And now everyone was out for the reward.

LORCAN

I let out a curse under my breath as all the people in the room slowly got to their feet, drawing their weapons, with wicked grins on their face.

Judging by their stares and the way Cintha was now looking at me with a slight tinge of fear in her eyes, I knew what had happened.

That bastard Brayden must've seen my fight with the giant creature and decided I was too much of a risk.

He'd changed my avatar to look like one of the monsters.

Fine.

I forced myself to stand up and face the approaching crowd.

My accelerated healing had already started working, but I still wasn't ready for a fight like this, not with the control it would take to keep the bloodshed to a minimum.

"Lorcan..." Cintha muttered, her voice low. "Don't.... Don't kill them, please?"

I nodded, letting her know I understood.

I was too tired to care much, even knowing they were likely as much victims as the rest of the trafficked humans.

Precision and control took more energy than wholesale slaughter.

When the first person ran in swinging his sword, I managed to catch his wrist and stop him from bringing it down, hitting him hard enough in the ribs to stun him so I could shove him aside before another came running at me.

My body was sluggish from the earlier battle, making it hard to fight. But I refused to give up, forced myself to keep going, no matter how much my body screamed at me.

Either the injuries were worse than I'd thought earlier, overpowering whatever dampeners Brayden had installed with his implant, or they'd found a way to reverse the effect, intensifying the existing pain.

Either way, I needed to find a way to end this fight soon.

"Stop it, everyone!" Cintha shouted over the sounds of the battle. Her voice was barely audible, and I doubted anyone else could hear her. "It's not real! He's another human like you. They're tricking you!"

I could hear the frustration in her voice, but there was nothing I could do to help her at this point.

Everyone here was too immersed in the illusion to believe it was real, that they were killing real things.

Besides, they all figured if they died, they'd just respawn.

The only way to get them to stop would be to turn off their implants somehow, but I only had the tools at my fingertips to remove them, and Cintha wouldn't approve.

Out of the corner of my eye, I saw her stumble, bracing herself against the table.

She didn't look injured, so I figured she must be trying to force her vision to switch, find a way to help, another exit, anything that would help us.

But for now, there was still a bloodthirsty mob pressing on us, laughing like this was the time of their lives.

I let the guy in the lead step closer before spinning him back, shoving him into the crowd to give us a little breathing room.

"Any time, love," I shouted while dancing away from the next, a giant of a woman who charged me, too focused to pay attention to my feint to the side.

"The lamp!"

Cintha yelled, and dove through the crowd.

In a long day of things that I didn't expect, that might be near the top.

Twisting and kicking, I followed her to the center of the room, eventually clearing the way by grabbing one of the tables and swinging it around me.

She climbed a chair, swinging at the large brightly colored lantern that hung from the center of the ceiling, but couldn't reach it.

"Lorcan, crush it!" She pointed.

That, I could manage. With a snarl, I released the table, letting it fly from my grip across the room toward the ceiling, then dove for Cintha, wrapping myself around her as we rolled to the floor.

An explosive crash rocked the room, then there was silence.

The tavern flickered out of view.

Everyone dropped their weapons and let out groans, their hands flying to their heads.

I had to grit my teeth to keep from dropping to my knees as the pain fully hit me all at once.

Void, it was going to take weeks to recover from these injuries, I thought as I fought to keep my legs from giving out.

Everyone looked around, confused, trying to figure out what was going on. The light in the cavern was much lower than it'd been in the illusion, only a few sparse domes on the wall illuminating the place.

The lantern.

The transmitter.

"Brilliant lady," I leaned over to wrap an arm around her, both to keep her close and maybe lean on her.

Just a little bit.

The dim light was enough to see everyone, see reality.

All the armor and silk were ragged, worn coveralls. The tall, muscled forms were gone, leaving them gaunt and wounded.

All their swords and hammers and whatever the hell someone had thought looked like a fun weapon had turned into pickaxes that now lay at their feet.

It was probably hard for them all to take in, but I knew we wouldn't have much time before Brayden realized his signal had been cut off.

I whistled loudly, the sound echoing off the stone walls. Everyone looked toward me, and I stood straight, ignoring the pain shooting through every inch of my body.

"In case you didn't notice, you've all been tricked. You're not playing some vid game, safe and sound in some pod. You had cybernetic implants installed into your heads." I tapped where I felt mine on the side of my temple. "They were overriding your senses, making you think everything you did, everything you saw or felt, was just a game. But it was all real."

Everyone started murmuring at once, trying to make sense of everything I said. I heard them whisper questions about the ones who'd died and hadn't ever respawned.

It sounded like some of the ones who'd "died" in the game hadn't been really dead and had been given medical attention before they "respawned."

Other's must've been beyond help and people just assumed they'd quit the game rather than respawning and losing their stuff.

Brayden and his crew really had thought of everything. No wonder the bastard had been so proud and smug.

None of us had ever suspected something like this might've been going on. We'd just assumed it was simple human trafficking, but this went way beyond all of that. I just hoped Brayden hadn't noticed Nixie.

I whistled again and waited until everyone's attention was back on me. "We're getting out of here before someone realizes we've broken their transmitter. It won't be long before they send people down to fix it and force us back into their game. If you want out, I suggest you follow us."

When I glanced over at Cintha, she nodded, then the

two of us turned and walked out of the cavern, down one of the winding tunnels.

Now that I had full access to all of my senses again, I was more than willing to trust my instincts.

At first, everyone stayed where they were. Then, slowly, they began to follow us, their footsteps echoing against the stone behind us.

I looked over at Cintha again and smiled. That had been a genius idea of hers, destroying the transmitter and shattering Brayden's illusion.

Without her, I'd have still been back there fighting.

Quite possibly losing.

Instead, I was able to reach down and take her hand.

I liked this option.

When we came to a crossroads, I stopped mid-step, holding up my hand for everyone to stop and stay silent. Closing my eyes, I took a deep breath and focused, listening for whatever it was that had made the hair on the back of my neck stand up. Then, after a brief moment, I heard it again. The same screeching sound the giant worm had made.

"Another one of those giant worms is coming," I told Cintha, keeping my voice low.

I wasn't thrilled with the thought of fighting another one of those things. Sure, I'd be able to see it, but I wasn't armed, and was far too injured.

I wouldn't be able to rely on the others to help me,

either, now that their illusion of being warriors had been shattered.

Our best bet was to keep moving and get out of the tunnels before it caught up with us. From what I could tell, it was still a bit away down one of the side tunnels. "Move quickly," I announced. "We're going to have company soon if we don't."

They all looked frightened, but nodded. Taking a deep breath, I headed straight ahead, picking up the pace. I couldn't wait to leave this place behind.

At first, the incline was barely noticeable, but it didn't take long before it was like walking up a steep cliffside. My body protested each and every step, but I still refused to give in.

Cintha was right there beside me, too, helping me each time I stumbled.

I wanted to get out of the cavern more than I wanted to sit and breathe.

A glance over my shoulder told me the others thought the same way. They were breathing heavily, but all had a look of grim determination on their faces.

Void knew how long they'd been down here, and I imagined they were all even more eager to get out than I was.

Eventually, the cavern turned to stairs.

But where would they lead to?

From the whispers back and forth through the

crowd, no one had any better ideas as to where we'd been taken.

Didn't have to be a forest planet, like I'd originally thought.

Anywhere with rock. Which left, oh, about one hundred percent of the universe.

It didn't matter.

We'd get out, get back to Orem, and then, when Cintha was safe, I'd make sure to be in for the kill when the Pack took out Brayden.

At the top of the stairs was a large door, locked and sealed to keep anyone from getting in and from getting out.

There was a keycard reader right next to the door, but apparently they'd searched us and taken the one I'd lifted off Horg's corpse. That would've just been too easy, and, honestly, probably wouldn't have worked.

It would have been nice for one single thing to be easy.

"How are we going to get out of here now?" Cintha asked, her hushed voice echoing down the stairwell.

I took a deep breath, closing my eyes and thinking. We could go back down and look for another way out, but I doubted we'd find one. Brayden would've found all the ways in and out of this place and sealed them all off.

He'd put too much thought into this operation to

overlook something as simple as that. Which meant we'd have to get through this door. Hacking into the card reader was an option, but I didn't know if anyone here had the skill to do such a thing.

Which meant forcing the door open.

"Everyone back up," I shouted.

Once everyone had gone back down a few steps, I backed up myself.

I wasn't quite healed up enough for this, but it wasn't like we had many options.

Again.

I charged up the steps, slamming my shoulder into the permasteel door. It shook, along with the stone surrounding it.

My shoulder ached, but the door still stood. I muttered a curse, then backed up and did it again, knowing everyone would be staring at me like I was insane.

Always possible.

Three more attempts, each jarring every bone in my body.

And then it burst open.

We'd done it.

We'd gotten out.

But where, exactly, was 'out'?

CINTHA

The moment we were in the corridor, people streamed out of the stairwell, running off in different directions.

I'd expected them to stay with us, to keep following, but now that they were out of the caves, it seemed like they'd been transformed into a herd of wild animals.

They scattered to the winds, going down the different halls, looking for Void knows what.

I turned in slow circles, almost certain I knew where we were.

The compound.

Brayden's compound.

"We were under it the entire time," I murmured.

"No wonder I didn't heal from the fight in the security room while they transferred us off the asteroid," Lorcan said, glaring at the corridors, as certain as I was. "We never left."

I looked through the crowd of people coming up behind us.

"Where is Daix?" I cried.

In the mob, I couldn't see him. Had he already passed us?

This was crazy. I'd have sworn I'd only seen fifty, maybe sixty, people down in the caverns, but it seemed like the flow of people was never-ending.

Had the implants kept us from seeing the additional players, as well?

I shook my head, furious. When would I be able to trust my own eyes again?

I grabbed a passing woman who looked vaguely like the tall fighter with the giant hammer I'd met in the tavern.

But now she was worn and gray, hair lank and stringy around her face. Shallow cuts ran down her arms and there were bruises under her eyes.

"Have you seen my brother?" I asked her. "The gamer I was talking to before?"

She stared around her, eyes wide, as if she couldn't hear me.

After so long in the game, how much of this new reality did she even see? Even believe?

Pushing me aside, she stumbled away, quickly lost in the stream.

I turned back to Lorcan. "Where could he have gone?"

He grabbed my hand so we couldn't be separated. "Daix is better off up here than down in the caverns," he insisted. "My brothers will be here soon, they'll be prepared for a full-scale retrieval."

"But I need to find him!"

"No," his face hardened. "We need to get to the shuttle bay with anyone else we can gather up, and get off this rock."

"I can't leave him," I insisted, my voice rising, shrill even to my own ears. "Not when I'm so close." I pulled away from him, searching the crowd.

For months I'd been searching, sending out messages, asking anyone and everyone with contacts or skills to see if they could find him.

And he'd been here, all this time, trapped in that damn game, not even knowing the danger he was in. I couldn't leave without him, not now.

The stream thinned. Still no sign of Daix.

I tore down the stairs. No one else was coming. He must have already gotten out when I wasn't looking, somehow, I'd missed him.

I looked around wildly. There was no telling where he could have ended up. I only knew a fraction of the space and who knew how many guards were still roaming the area.

Oh Void, we should have kept the pickaxes. Anything would be better than wandering around completely unarmed.

My thoughts whirled madly until Lorcan grabbed my shoulders.

"We have to leave," he insisted. "The rest of the team will be here soon, and I promise you they'll search for him, find him. But we'd be chasing our tails if we just kept wandering blindly."

He must have seen the desolation on my face. "Come on, maybe he's already made his way to the shuttle bay."

"Maybe," I sniffed.

He was right. I knew he was right.

But it felt like giving up at the last moment.

We hadn't taken more than three steps before Nika came crashing into my arms.

"We can at least get you out," I swore to her. "How did you escape? Did the prisoners find a way to open up the factory floors?"

Her wide eyes searched my face frantically, "No," she stuttered, lips pale, "that's not what happened."

From around the corner, Teldra stepped, blaster in hand.

"I think what she means to say is, I came and fetched her."

I really, really didn't understand.

My mind grabbed for the one thing that possibly made sense.

"You got free, too! Good, come on!"

I reached for Teldra, but she backed up and raised the blaster.

"You are so predictable. Sweet, but predictable. Back to me, girl," she snapped.

Head lowered, Nika shuffled back to Teldra's side.

This was it. The final question that I just couldn't figure out.

"What's going on?"

I stared at them blankly until Lorcan stepped to my side, waves of anger radiating from him.

"What's going on is that our gracious hostess has slapped a new bit of jewelry on your friend."

I finally saw it. A dark gray choker wrapped around Nika's neck.

I shook my head. "I don't understand, what does that have to do with anything? Why aren't we leaving?"

"It's there to buy me a little thinking time," Teldra hissed. "It took long enough for your merry band to make its way out of the caverns. Plenty of time to review the tapes from when you were on the work floor, find a pressure point." She shrugged at Nika. "Not a particularly interesting one, but I'll use whatever I need to."

"I'm so sorry," Nika's eyes watered as she clawed at the band around her neck. "I didn't realize what she was putting on me."

"It's ugly," I started, "but--"

"It's wired to blow," Lorcan explained. "Teldra wants our help for something, that should make sure she gets it."

Blood drained from my face, and I shivered as I stared at the evil-looking gray band cutting into Nika's delicate flesh.

"You didn't need to do this." I turned to Teldra. "We would have helped you get out of here anyway, helped you escape."

"Love," Lorcan rubbed my shoulder. "She was never a prisoner here."

Every idea I'd had about my time here, every theory, it all shattered, the pieces reassembling like a mosaic, turned upside down and backwards to reveal a new picture.

"Teldra, there you are!" Brayden staggered down the hall towards us, eyes fixed on her. His hair stuck out every which way, his clothing was disheveled, and he had a dark smear down his face as if he'd run into something unpleasant.

Gone was the self-assured, disgustingly jovial man who had gladly handed me over to his friends.

At the dinner table, at the horrible, stilted meals, he'd been oblivious to everything other than the story he told himself.

Now, it looked like reality was starting to break through.

"Teldra," he continued again, "what's going on? I can't find anyone, and I would've sworn I saw product roaming the hallways."

Product.

People. Any flash of sympathy I might've had for him was squashed.

"Section six is completely off-line," he continued rambling. "And I can't pull up cameras on seven or eight."

"Yes, Brayden. I'm aware."

"And I've gone over all the records, but I can't find out what happened with Horg or Durl." His voice rose, pitch becoming shrill. "And the rest of the team isn't reporting."

Teldra's face didn't twitch, she didn't even raise an eyebrow as he continued ranting at her.

"Yes, Brayden. I'm aware," she repeated.

We stood frozen, unable to run, forced to let them

play out their weird sibling drama because of the damn choker on Nika's neck.

"Are you sure about the choker?" I whispered to Lorcan. "She likes mind games, it might not be real."

He shook his head. "I can smell the explosives." The ghost of a smile lifted the corner of his lips. "It's at least as real as anything else we've dealt with lately."

I closed my eyes while Brayden chattered away at his sister, demanding she explain, fix things, make it better.

A giggle, horribly, terribly inappropriate bubbled up through my chest.

I pressed my hands over my lips, trying to keep it down, but it burst through, startling me with the sound.

This was absurd. All of it was ridiculous. At any moment, I expected to be back down in the weird fantasy tavern. I looked down at my gray, torn coveralls.

"I think I liked that dress," I finally said aloud. "What did you think?"

A bright smile broke through Lorcan's grim demeanor. "It did have a teasing little slit ride about there." His finger grazed my hip, and even now, even here, sparks ran through me at his touch. "After all this, let's get you one. A real one, this time. Maybe a closetful, so I don't have to worry about ripping them off you."

"I see." I smiled back, lips pressed tightly together to hold back another inappropriate laugh.

Yes, we really were insane.

Yes, the woman with a blaster who apparently held the remote for the explosive device around my friend's neck was standing there deflecting questions from her slave-trading brother, who apparently had become hysterical.

But you know what, there wasn't much else to do.

"When we get out of this," I called across to Nika, still captive beside Teldra's, "wanna come back with me to Orem?"

Her eyes were like saucers. Obviously, she thought we'd gone around the bend, too.

"I'm thinking of expanding the shop," I continued, "and it would be nice to--"

Brayden finally noticed us.

"You!" he exclaimed.

All right, he noticed Lorcan. "This is all your fault," he cried.

He stalked down the corridor, away from Teldra and her bored expression, hands twisted into claws reaching for Lorcan, spittle flying with every word.

"You killed my men, you set those explosives, you--"

"No, brother dear." Teldra's voice cut through his rising shouts.

"That would've been me."

He turned back to face her, spine rigid with shock.

And without another word, she shot him, clear through the chest.

He collapsed midway down the corridor, and finally she smiled.

"I've really been looking forward to that."

LORCAN

Over the years there had been any number of missions that had gone slightly pear-shaped. Even more than slightly.

This would have to be added to the top of that list.

But at least I had pleasant company for it, even if I wished Cintha a million miles away from here, somewhere safe.

Teldra jerked Nika back towards her, reminding us, as if the body on the floor wasn't quite enough, that she was in charge here.

She sighed, as if a little disappointed. "I did plan to drag everything out a bit longer, watching him spiral down was amusing."

I'd thought her bored, remote. Honestly that was a lot less disconcerting than when she was amused.

She continued, "Take away his guards, his friends, his safety." Her lips pursed. "But you've ruined my timeline, and I am sincerely annoyed with you all."

She'd gestured down the hall with the blaster. "Come on, I need to think."

With prodding, Cintha took her place at the front of our little procession.

"You next, soldier boy," Teldra said. "I'll keep her little friend back with me. Remember, nothing will take long to trigger if I get nervous."

Cintha nodded, face pale, all of her brave joking of moments earlier swept aside as she headed away.

With a jolt, I realized Cintha actually knew where to go.

Interesting, but I wasn't sure how to make use of it. Not yet.

"I knew Brayden couldn't have been the one behind all of this," I spoke over my shoulder, voice casual, nonthreatening. "Never seemed like he had the brains."

"I did worry it would be obvious," she commented mildly. "But most people are perfectly happy to go with the obvious man-in-charge.

After a few minutes of uneasy silence, Cintha stopped halfway down the corridor, in front of yet another door.

"It won't open for me."

"Of course not." Teldra dragged Nika up with her,

then shoved her into Cintha, making both women stumble slightly.

I tensed, but there was still no way to safely take her down, not without casualties that Cintha would find unacceptable.

Now that I knew what I was dealing with, however, there would be a way.

There always was.

The door slid open.

"Inside," Teldra ordered.

Once again, Cintha led the way, with me close behind.

Teldra stayed by the door, tapped the control panel once, then twice.

The low hum of electronics tipped me that the door had now been sealed. And then the outer wall began to open.

The outer screens slowly irised to reveal reinforced plex, so clear as to be transparent despite its thickness, opening the room to the starscape beyond.

With a shriek, Nika shrank back, the younger girl obviously having been pushed just a bit further than she could cope.

Just what I needed.

Living on stations and outer colonies, not many people had to confront the cold, empty void.

A large fraction of them couldn't handle it, just

broke down when they first saw the vastness, the unending black immensity of it all.

How tiny and insignificant they were, all of us were, in comparison.

And it looked like Nika might be one of those.

Fantastic.

"It's all right," Cintha soothed her, her voice calm and easy, though she flicked a quick glance at Teldra. "It's perfectly safe. This is just her thinking place. You don't have to look outside if you don't want to."

With slow steps, she approached the shivering girl, whose eyes were still fixed in horrified absorption at the expense without.

"Don't look," Cintha whispered, and turned Nika away from the plex.

"Well, that's another happy little twist." Teldra threw herself into one of the chairs, eyes searching the starscape outside for something.

And with the sudden flash of a smile, I knew her clever, twisted brain had found it.

"You may as well sit," she waved one hand, ever the hostess. "You're not going anywhere for a while."

I perched on the edge of a chair, glad her attention was on me instead of Cintha.

At least for now.

"So, what are you? Some sort of new Imperial trooper?"

"Not exactly. More of a free agent."

Which, even though we had our secret treaty with the Empire in place, was the truth.

I might be investigating the trafficking as a favor for Loree's friend, who apparently happened to be the Imperial heir, but that didn't mean I was one of his soldiers.

Besides, favor for the Empire or not, none of us approved of what they'd been doing here. It was a pleasure to help take it down.

Fingers tapping on the arm of the chair, she didn't look at me, her eyes moving restlessly from one distant star to the next.

"My systems caught the edge of your signal, you know." More tapping, almost like typing whatever was flying through her mind. "Didn't crack it, which was interesting in itself, but the fact that signal even existed was enough to tell me it was time to accelerate my timeline."

The knife that had twisted in my gut relaxed, but only a fraction.

I'd been counting on Nixie to get the signal through. And now, I couldn't be completely sure.

"But I'd still bet you've got back-up on the way," she mused. "And I don't know how far out they are. So, I think we'll wait for them to join the party."

Damn.

She must've caught the flare of my nostrils from her peripheral vision. "Don't worry, I haven't mined the shuttle bay. I think I want to borrow a little something once they get here."

"What makes you think they're going to cooperate?" I asked, reluctantly impressed. She had no morals, didn't seem at all concerned about the slavery she'd sent however many thousands of people into, but still, a brilliant, if twisted, mind lay behind those placid eyes.

Doc would've loved her.

"They'll want you. And you want her." She pointed at Cintha. "And she wants her, alive and unharmed." She ended by pointing the blaster at Nika, who had curled up into a shaking ball.

"Void knows why." Her lip curled, annoyed. "But she and I will be taking a little trip. After I make sure I won't be followed."

A low moan from Nika.

Cintha turned, lips pressed into a thin line. "Why would you take her? You'll regret it before you even leave atmosphere."

Teldra gazed at her appraisingly "You're right, you know. And I underestimated you. You even told me you noticed details. I just didn't realize how good you were."

Cintha shook her head. "You were the one who built the game, weren't you?"

A feral flash of teeth. "A generative, adaptive, full-sensory-immersion virtual reality construct. With minimal monitoring, it could run forever, make adjustments for any environmental change, shift in player capabilities, anything."

"It was never about the trafficking, was it?" Cintha wondered aloud.

I pushed down with my hand, frantically wishing she'd be quiet, let me keep Teldra's attention away from her.

Keep her safe.

"Not originally. But you have no idea how expensive my materials are." Teldra shrugged. "It was a way for the program to pay for itself."

"Now what?"

"Now we're going to wait.

Cintha rose to her feet in one fluid motion. "Take me with you instead," she demanded.

"No!" I shouted but the women ignored me.

Teldra tilted her head to the side. "You'd be less annoying, that's true. But if I take you, he's going to be more motivated to track me down."

That was the understatement of the millennium.

If she did one thing to harm Cintha, the there was no place in the Empire or the Fringe or any place else humans sucked air, that I wouldn't go to tear her to shreds.

"That's one way to think of it," Cintha shrugged,

deliberately oblivious to my turmoil. "Or you could think that he'd be more motivated to convince whoever his friends are to leave you alone."

Teldra got up and stood near the window, hand appearing pressed against the stars.

"It's possible," she mused. "It will take time to reestablish, rebuild."

"Considering what you got done here tethered to that idiot," Cintha forced a laugh, "I'm sure you'd manage, somehow."

"That's true," Telstra didn't turn, just watched the stars.

I shook my head at Cintha, for the first time wishing for a mental bond like the one Eris and Connor shared.

Stop talking to her, I mentally shouted at Cintha. Stop proposing crazy things. I'll figure this out.

Cintha, of course, wasn't having any of it.

Hell, she wouldn't, even if she could hear me.

She stepped a little closer to Telstra, easing herself between the window and Nika.

"You wouldn't be starting from scratch, at least."

"No, I suppose this could be considered something of a test run. Fairly successful, with some hiccups." She nodded, the temporary softness turning to resolve again. "I'll do better next time."

She turned, studying Nika on the floor like a scientist about to dissect some poor hapless amphibian.

"You're right. She'd be deadweight. I'm already annoyed by the sniveling."

"Then give me the remote," Cintha said hastily.

"Oh love, she's not going to do that."

"Your boyfriend's right," Teldra replied. "If you're coming with me, you'll be wearing the choker."

Cintha paled slightly, then nodded. "That's fine."

No, it wasn't.

Not fine, not at all.

And there wasn't a damn thing I could do about it.

"I'm assuming there's a way to take it off her without harming her? Because if there's not, no deal."

Teldra rolled her eyes. "Of course. Check the back of the collar."

Cintha knelt down, one hand slowly rubbing Nika's shoulders, while the other lifted her hair up to expose the seam of the choker.

"Carefully, very carefully I'd suggest, slide the plate to the left," Teldra instructed, blaster aimed solidly at Nika's head.

Cintha did so, revealing a tiny keypad. "Now what?"

But whatever Teldra was about to say was interrupted by a cheerful blare through the room's speakers.

Hi, everybody! I think I should help now.

"No!" I roared back.

"They're here," Teldra growled. "Hurry up. I

wouldn't hit the wrong key, you're far too close. Technically, we all are."

I froze. If Cintha miskeyed, if Nika flinched, the explosion would kill them both.

Slowly, Teldra recited the code.

Cintha painstakingly entered each digit.

The room filled with the scent of blood. I glanced down, noticing Nika had made fists so tight that her nails cut into her palms in her effort to stay still.

Brave girl, and hopefully not a soon-to-be-dead one.

"Soldier boy," Teldra snapped. "Since your control officer seems to be patched into our announcement system, let them know we'll be heading to the shuttle bay soon. I want our path to be cleared. No surprises."

I swallowed, throat tight, but complied.

Sort of. "Control, did you hear that?"

Trusting Nixie was always a dicey affair.

She was seldom actually malicious, but sometimes didn't understand the finer parts of human, or close-to-human behavior.

Such as subterfuge.

And lying.

Both of which would be remarkably useful skills right now.

With a ping, she came back on the line.

Sure thing, soldier boy. I'll let them know!

Well, whatever she was going to do, Teldra at least

didn't seem to be suspicious of Nixie's behavior.

Maybe she thought all imperial officers sounded like that.

Do you need anything else? Nixie chirped.

I looked at Teldra, who shook her head.

"No, that's enough for now. Thanks for keeping an ear out."

She was listening. That was a start.

And if Nixie was listening, with luck, she'd taken control of the rest of the complex's systems.

And hopefully the rest of the team was on their way, maybe even in close orbit.

"Now that the interruptions are over, are you ready for the second set of codes?" Teldra drawled.

Cintha nodded, face tight, all her focus on the tiny keypad that controlled both her and the girl's life.

She entered number after number until, finally, a soft click sounded, like a slamming door to my ears.

"Is it right?" Cintha barely breathed the words.

"Only one way to find out," Teldra barked with a bitter laugh. "Pull it off her."

Cintha's hands gripped the edge of the choker, her eyes closed tight.

"Lorcan, if something happens, promise me you'll keep an eye on Talley. Don't tell her what happened, don't let her blame herself."

Nothing was going to happen.

Nothing

I wouldn't let it.

But that wasn't what she needed to hear.

"Of course," I ground out through gritted teeth.

"Enough with the stalling. It doesn't sound like a ship's landed yet, and I don't plan to let them get too far ahead of me. Time's a-wasting."

"All right, Nika," Cintha whispered to her, still worried for the girl. "I'm going to do this fast, and then you go to Lorcan, alright?"

"One."

I could see the lines of tension run down her fingers as she stiffened, bracing herself.

"Two."

Nika's eyes closed, tears running down her cheeks.

"Three!"

Cintha swooped her arms in front of Nika's throat, clearing the choker away.

Nothing happened.

"Good job." Teldra stepped back towards the window, blaster still aimed at Nika's head but all her attention now on Cintha. "Your turn."

No.

It was *my* turn.

"Nixie, open the door now!" I snapped, lunging across the room, blocking Teldra's line of fire as I grabbed the explosive choker, crushing it in my hand.

The echo of my words still rang in the room as the door slid open.

Cintha looked back at me, but I shook my head. "Get her out of here!"

She reached down and dragged the crying girl behind her into the corridor.

I caught a glance of her worried face before I turned away. There was business to be finished here.

"Seal it, Nixie," I ordered.

The subtle change in pressure let me know she'd complied.

If Nixie had control of the station and my brothers were on the way, nothing could hurt Cintha now.

With that knowledge, the last worry fell from me.

I stared at Teldra, still standing proudly before the field of stars.

"It was brilliant," I admitted. "But you had to have known it was wrong."

She shrugged. "It doesn't seem like many people are as concerned about that as you seem to be. What will you do now?"

Despite everything, her voice was calm, even.

No fear.

"I wasn't planning on bringing back prisoners, but plans change. Certainly have with this mission."

"I am glad I didn't bore you."

I couldn't help but smile. "You would've gotten

along well with the ladies back home," I nodded with grudging respect. "At least half of them are, shall we say, as morally ambiguous as you?"

"Shame I'll never meet them." She pulled her hand away from her side, displaying the remote she still held. "And you won't be seeing them again, either."

I charged towards her, but not in time to stop the click of the button.

I flung the choker towards the window, away from Cintha.

The concussion shook the room, throwing the chairs about.

When it was over, Teldra was slumped in a corner half under a chair, blood trickling from her forehead, eyes fixed, unseeing, on the stars.

It was over.

All of it was over.

Now to get back to Cintha, help her find her brother and get the prisoners off this nightmare planetoid.

CRACK.

The sound shattered the stillness.

And then another crack.

And another.

Until the entire sheet of plexi was covered by a web of them.

And in a moment, it blew.

CINTHA

"**L**orcan!" I screamed, pounding on the door panel. The explosion had shattered the air, shaking the entire corridor.

But then there was nothing but silence.

"Whoever you are, open this door!" I shouted.

I'm sorry. Cintha, do you mind if I call you Cintha? I think we're going to be friends. We should be friends. But I can't open it right now. Besides he wouldn't like it, and, whether or not he realizes it, I like Lorcan.

I blinked, shaking my head.

This wasn't some seasoned mission operative.

She sounded almost like Talley.

Well, before Talley hit that sulky age.

"Look, whoever you are," I said firmly, "you're going

to open that door and you're going to let me take care of Lorcan."

No reply.

"Do it right now, missie."

I'm not missie. I'm Nixie!

A tickle in my brain, something Lorcan had said, but too much had happened and I couldn't pull it up.

Really, I think we'd be best if you came this way, the others are landing and they'll explain it better. Well, not better, but sometimes people don't seem to understand when I'm explaining it. Do you think it's because I don't have a body? I'd like to have a body, just for a day or two.

I pulled a stunned Nika off the floor, and together we followed the sounds of the chattering child's voice through the empty compound.

By flashing lights and her voice coming from the speakers ahead of us, she led us to the shuttle bay.

Apparently, she'd led everyone there. It was filled with prisoners from the assembly lines, the gamers we'd been trapped with, hundreds of people, most I'd never seen.

But all of them looked stunned, surprised and wary of whatever was going to happen next.

The shuttle bay held three ships I didn't recognize, they hadn't been here when we'd been taken off the transport...

Was it really only a few days ago?

And standing head-and-shoulders above the crowd were faces I recognized from the patrols through the Under back on Orem. Big men, tough. Somehow, rough and wild-looking.

Lorcan's brothers.

My hand tight around Nika's wrist so we didn't get separated, I shoved through the throng, desperate to reach one of them, any of them.

Surely, they'd be able to tell me what was going on, be able to tell me Lorcan was all right.

"Hey, there you are!"

Daix grabbed me, pulled me into a tight hug. "Still wrapping my brain around this whole thing. Crazy, isn't it." His easy smile shocked me, made me wonder if he'd actually paid attention to what had happened to him, to me. "Where'd you go? Lost sight of you along the way. Weren't you with that guy?"

"This is not the time for us to catch up," I snapped.

He stepped back, eyes actually focused on me, and I realized I probably should've taken that tone with him years ago.

"Yeah, but I just wanted to help --"

"You want to help? Here." I put Nika's hand in his.

"You take care of her," I demanded. "You take care of her like she was the most precious thing on the planet, get her medical care, get her food, make sure she gets out of here and back to Orem."

I turned to Nika, mind still racing. Where was Lorcan? "Is that alright with you? I just need to-"

Without warning, she hugged me. "Go, see what you can find out. And thank you. Thank you both."

She stepped back towards Daix, who looked on in confusion.

"I mean it, don't screw up this time," I stressed, then kept working through the crowd.

I pressed on towards the closest of Lorcan's brothers, the one I thought I'd seen with Loree.

He was directing the swarm of people to different corners, at first look triaging them by the severity of their wounds.

That was great, but I needed him right now.

Everyone else would have to wait.

"Hey!" I shouted, then my brain blanked. Name. Name.

Screw it.

"Lorcan's brother!"

His head whipped towards me, eyes meeting mine.

"I know you," he smiled. "Loree's friend, right? Void, she's going to be pissed you were here. Let's get you checked out and--"

"The hell with that, where is he? Where's Lorcan?"

His brow furrowed. "He's on base somewhere, I'm sure. Trust me, he's good at this kind of stuff."

"You don't understand," I pushed out, shaking with

the effort not to scream. "There was an explosion. He stopped answering me. I think," my mind went to that expanse of stars twinkling just outside the plex, "I think he might have been blown outside the complex."

His jaw tightened. "Let me check." He tapped a patch behind his ear, some sort of comm unit, spoke with a pitch so low and quickly I couldn't make out his words, just waited, fists flexing, desperate to do something, hear something.

He couldn't have saved me, and then be just gone, could he?

"Ronan says for me to take you to Doc, alright? I'm Xander, by the way. Seems like we should have meet officially by now."

A doctor? I asked, my brain just not able to keep up. Maybe the last few days had finally caught up with me.

I stared at the crowd blankly. Without Lorcan, I didn't want to go anywhere.

"Hey," Xander bent down until his face was level with mine. "You've had a bad time of it here, but if I don't get you over to Doc, safe and sound, there's going to be a line of folks waiting to kick my ass." He tilted his head, looked a bit goofy. "Starting with Loree. So, help me out a bit?"

Another tall, broad man took his place, directing the crowd. Xander nodded, then guided me through, his hand resting just over my shoulder.

People melted away from us or, more likely, my guide, leaving an open path to the far corner where an elderly lady in a lab coat had set up a makeshift clinic.

"Doc, this is Cintha."

"Lorcan's girl?" Her eyes flashed with an uncomfortable level of excitement. "You'll have to take it for now, Nadira."

She tossed a datapad to another woman who caught it with a roll of the eyes and an ease that bespoke long practice. "I want to meet this one before any of you poison her mind against me."

Wait.

What?

"Doc, you know we love you," the other woman laughed as she turned to the next patient. "We just wonder about your babysitting skills."

"Vicki loves me the most," the older woman said with a fierce look in her eye.

"Of course she does," Xander laughed. "Because you've never told her no."

Doc grabbed my hand, not-at-all discreetly checking my pulse while staring at my pupils. "You've had a rough time of it. Looks like you've got one of those bitch's toys in your head." She grinned. "I'll get that taken care of, don't worry about it. Looking forward to seeing how it works. Come with me, sweetie."

I pulled back.

"I'm not going anywhere until someone tells me what's going on."

Locking my hands in front of my chest, I planted my feet, refused to move, took every bit of strength until someone, anyone would listen to me.

"Where. Is. Lorcan?"

Warm, strong arms slid around me from behind, pulled me back into a fierce embrace.

"Right here, love," he murmured into my hair.

"Dammit. I'm never going to get my side of the story in first," Doc stomped off. "Both of you, come see me as soon as you're done canoodling."

"Canoodling?" I wondered, blinking at her retreating form.

"Yeah, meet Doc," Lorcan answered. "You learn to just roll with it."

Xander slapped Lorcan on the shoulder. "Welcome back. Now, go make her happy, or she'll take it out on us all."

He faded back into the crowd as I turned in the safely of Lorcan's embrace.

"What happened?" I gasped. Cuts ran all over his face and arms, smears of blood already drying.

"Nothing terrible," he lifted me up, nuzzled into my neck as if he couldn't get enough of my scent.

"I'm serious," I insisted. Not immediately. But eventually.

He sighed, put me down, but didn't let me go.

"The plexi blew."

I shuddered. It was everything I'd refused to imagine as we'd limped towards the shuttle bay, every image my stupid imagination kept throwing at me.

But here he was.

Fine.

Well, mostly fine.

"How?"

He didn't need any more of a question. "Nixie got the shielding down. Not immediately, but soon enough."

It could have gone so very, very wrong. The tears that had threatened for the last long minutes started to spill.

He brought his hand to my cheek, wiped one away. "It's alright now, it's over."

I grabbed his hand, staring at his fingers. The fingertips down to the first knuckle were shredded, as if he'd planted them into the permisteel itself to hold on.

"I'll explain everything," he promised. "I'm safe, and you're safe." He glanced up, a half-grin lifting his lips. "But if we want to stay that way, I'd suggest we don't make Doc wait any longer."

EPILOGUE: CINTHA

"Where should I put this?" Talley yelled across the shop as she held up a golden bracelet.

It was one of the ones she'd made for a client while I'd been gone, and she was very proud of the work she'd done.

And I was very proud of how she'd managed to keep things running without me.

She'd continued on pretty well for a girl her age, even working on the smaller projects that came in, while leaving the big ones for me.

She'd done a good job at estimating her skills.

Either that, or she'd done well hiding her failures.

Either way, I was a well-pleased aunt.

"Put it in one of the small black boxes and give it to

Nika to wrap," I instructed, only glancing away for a moment from the necklace I was inlaying jewels into.

Nika had taken me up on my wild offer made in that corridor. Ever since getting back to Orem, she'd been my right hand.

And with all the work I had piled up for me when I got back, I definitely needed the help. Having Nika there meant she could handle most of the non-jeweler work around the shop - packaging the items, talking with customers, that sort of thing.

Which freed me up to work on the complex projects, and Talley to take care of the simpler ones.

Daix had been around to take care of the deliveries I needed done and to handle retrieving the materials I'd ordered. During his downtime, Daix had been working with Lorcan and his brothers.

Well, not exactly working with, but introducing them around the Under, helping them figure out who was part of the system here, and who were predators who needed to go.

All of us were trying to keep him busy, keep him working and out of trouble.

Sure, he hadn't meant to get sucked into Brayden and Teldra's game, but it had still cost him years of his daughter's life.

I wasn't about to let him out of my sight for a while.

Even if I suspected that Nika was half the reason he kept coming by so often.

When the chime above the door jingled, I couldn't help but look up, despite knowing Nika was handling the customers just fine.

But I was glad I did, since it wasn't a customer that walked in.

Lorcan.

After everything, after we'd been back for weeks, just seeing him made my mouth dry and my chest tighten.

And started a few other little flutters.

"I'll be with you in a second, love," I told Lorcan as I finished setting the last of the gems. The necklace looked beautiful, but not quite perfect.

It was a recreation of the one I'd seen in Teldra's jewelry cabinet, but I wasn't completely satisfied with how it looked.

Still, it would more than surpass what the woman who ordered it had requested, and it was time to close up for the day.

Once I had it safely put away, I walked over to Lorcan and wrapped my arms around him, burying my head against his chest.

He chuckled and hugged me back, his arms tight and strong around me. Void, it felt good to be with him without the fear of death lingering over us.

"How are you doing?" he asked, just as he did every time he came into the shop. He hadn't quite moved in with me yet. Not officially.

But that didn't stop him from coming by after his shift every day.

And I couldn't remember the last night he hadn't spent at my side.

"Just perfect," I said, smiling up at him.

And it was the truth. I'd had a mean headache for a few days after Lorcan's Doc had removed the implant from my head, but now it was all healed up, without even a scar to show where it had been.

Everyone who'd been rescued from the caverns had had theirs removed as well, making sure no one could tap into the system Teldra had designed and control them again.

Since we'd gotten back, Lorcan had filled me in on a lot of his past, answering so many questions I'd had.

I was sure he still had a few secrets of his own, but I'd figure them all out in time, just as he'd figure out all of mine.

But those were easy, natural secrets, the kind that made every relationship an adventure. And not the trying-to-kill-us kind of adventure. I'd had my fill of that for forever.

When I stood on my toes to press my lips to Lorcan's, the sound of gagging came from behind me. I turned and glared at Talley, who just rolled her eyes at me.

"Can't you two get a room or something?" she complained.

Apparently, sticking my tongue out at her wasn't the grown-up thing to do, but who cared. I'd been responsible enough for a while.

"I'll lock up," Nika offered, a knowing smile on her lips.

I turned back to Lorcan, took his hand in mine, and started pulling him toward the stairs. "Come on," I said "you heard the girl. Let's go upstairs and find ourselves a room."

He grinned back at me while Nika snickered. Talley, on the other hand, just made even louder gagging sounds combined with utterances of "Ew!" and "Gross!"

Void, it was good to be home.

LETTER FROM ELIN

C oming back to the world of the Pack is always so much fun!

I missed them all, but writing Nixie is a special joy :)

In the next few months we'll be seeing more of our growly boys, so make sure you don't miss anything.

Be sure you've either signed up for my newsletter, have joined the facebook group, or both!

And please don't forget to leave a review. I love reading what you think of the books!

XOXO,

. . .

Elin

P.S. KEEP READING for the first bit of Vrehx, book one of my alien romance series, Conquered World!

PLEASE DON'T FORGET TO LEAVE A REVIEW!

R eaders rely on your opinions, and your review can help others decide on what books they read. Make sure your opinion is heard and leave a review where you purchased this book!

DON'T MISS A NEW RELEASE! You can sign up for release alerts at both Amazon and Bookbub:
bookbub.com/authors/elin-wyn
amazon.com/author/elinwyn

FOR A FREE SHORT STORY, opportunities for advance review copies, release news and the occasional cat picture, please join the newsletter!

https://elinwynbooks.com/newsletter-signup/

AND DON'T FORGET the Facebook group, where I post sneak peeks of chapters and covers!

https://www.facebook.com/groups/ElinWyn/

DON'T MISS THE CONQUERED
WORLD!

He shattered her world. Can she trust him with her heart?

Giant spiders, walking trees, bloodthirsty vines.

For Jeneva, it's just another day trying to survive in the jungles of Ankau.

Until the sky ripped open, and the true monsters came through.

Now her world is under attack, and the only place of safety may be at the side of a rock-hard scaled alien.

But he's filled with secrets - how can she trust him?

Vrehx cares for nothing other than the destruction of the Xathi hordes who burned his home and killed his family.

But when a weapons test goes horribly wrong, the battle spills over to an uncharted world.

The planet is filled with lethal native life...but nothing is more dangerous than the human woman who obsesses his thoughts.

When war rages around them, can they fight together, or will his burning need for her drive them apart?

Vrehx is the first book in the science fiction romance series Conquered World. Each book is a new romance with alpha male alien warriors and women who don't put up with their nonsense. No cheating, no cliffhangers, HEA guaranteed!

Click to get Vrehx now or keep reading for a sample!
https://elinwynbooks.com/conquered-world-alien-romance/

VREHX

Streaks of plasma lit the blackness as a squadron of Valorni fighters swooped in dizzying spirals, blasting at the massive Xathi ship that filled the screens of the *Vengeance*.

We were so close it was the size of a planet. Like two steel ziggurats smashed and welded together. Not practical for space flight, but efficient enough to tear through several worlds.

Designed to intimidate.

Designed to destroy.

And we were going to stop it.

We crept closer, waiting. I sucked in my breath, geared for the inevitable.

I gritted my teeth as the bridge shook, and Karzin let out an undignified whoop from his station on the far curve of the bridge. The purple stripes on his shoulders rippled, and his excited eyes darted back and forth as if cheering on his favorite sport.

Barbarian. His crude Valorni traits got on my last nerve—not that he gave a rat's ass. Like the lot of them, he had no empathy for others. He barely listened to commands and forget anyone who didn't at least match his rank.

"You green motherfuckers aren't supposed to be hitting us, just laying cover for our approach," I snarled. "They can remember that much, can't they?"

They had only begun venturing into space when we took them into the alliance, but surely they weren't that stupid.

I hoped not.

"Fuck you," the Valorni drawled. The stretched-out

sounds of his abominable accent were like bristles to my red Skotan scales. "Not their fault we're cloaked all to hell."

What an asshole. Valorni couldn't even be bothered to speak accurately. Their drawl made it nearly impossible to understand them, and they had idiotic slang for everything.

"They were informed of our flight path before the battle." The lights of Sk'lar's implants flickered in the dim light of the bridge. "It should have been simple for them to avoid it."

I smiled just a little, glad I wasn't the only one with some common sense. Sk'lar wasn't much better than Karzin, but he was more tolerable. My biggest problem was his implants.

His artificial augmentation was just creepy and wrong. You could see them light up in biohazard green against his shiny black skin. He looked like a fucking motherboard.

The strike team leaders were chosen for their specific talents and leadership, but Sk'lar's was not stealth outside the ship.

Karzin made it a point to butt heads with all of us. That usually distracted the rest of us from being at each other's throats.

Maybe that was his intention. Whatever. He was an asshole.

Karzin shrugged off the K'ver's barely concealed criticism. "Not gonna matter in a few minutes, is it?"

The sarcasm warranted him a disapproving side-eye from Sk'lar, which he ignored. I hated to admit it, but the jackass was right. In a few minutes, we would probably all be dead.

"Gentlemen," Rouhr's quiet word from the command station silenced the chatter, "are you prepared?"

The scar that ran down the left side of his face rippled as he clenched his jaw. He was annoyed.

Of course, we were prepared.

We shut up anyway. Rouhr was very diplomatic. That's why he was in charge.

We straightened ourselves and regained our concentration.

Tension and anger clogged the air, but there was no fear. Fear had died when our families did, when our worlds had burned under the Xathi attacks.

Around the half circle, each of us activated the new weapons panels, the long seconds drawing out as they lit up and hummed. Every battle had this moment—the waiting before the storm.

But this would be different.

We owned the storm.

"Let's blow a hole in those bastards," I growled, eyes

fixed on the sickly green hull, thinking of the swarms inside.

They waited for the go ahead to surge through over the squadrons like locusts.

Nothing had been able to penetrate a Xathi hiveship before. They just plowed through and destroyed whatever they wanted, the swarms mopping up whatever the hiveship missed.

The Valorni, as annoying as they were, were inducted into the alliance for one reason. The Sugavians had worked with K'ver scientists using codialite, a mineral from the Valorni homeworld, to make one last attempt.

Just enough had been mined for this last-ditch effort —an experimental weapon that had a shot at penetrating that hull. It was rare, and we were on the losing end of this fight. We only had one shot.

We'd better make it count.

Every Skotan, K'ver, and Valorni warrior on the *Vengeance* had volunteered in the knowledge that it was a one-way trip. If this worked, the three strike teams below would board the Xathi and battle until there was nothing left.

If it didn't, we'd all die—just sooner.

Either way, the recorder satellites would beam the results of the experiment back to the scientists and engineers. We'd succeed, or they'd build a better weapon next time. That was the most important part of the mission, and we all understood how expendable we were.

The three of us locked focus on our stations as we crept closer.

"We are now in firing range, Captain," Sk'lar reported.

"Fire at will," was the only response.

Karzin sent the signal to the Valorni ships, and I started a slow count.

One.

His comrades had fought stupidly but bravely. There was no discernable pattern to the attack.

I was worried more would take friendly fire than would hit the Xathi, but they somehow made sense of the chaos, dodging fire from their comrades. If any survived the battle, they deserved to escape.

Two.

More likely the crazy bastards would follow us into the breach, but they'd earned the choice.

Three.

I activated the launch panel and braced, eyes fixed on the monitors. The adrenaline rushed through me in anticipation of the blow.

Nothing.

Not a bang or a pop or a whine. Just the hum of the

engines, and the wall of the Xathi ship growing larger on the screens.

The anticipation deflated as I looked at the panel in confusion. The damn thing was experimental, but it should at least fire. The engineers weren't brain-dead.

With a snarl, I slapped it again.

And then the universe turned inside out.

JENEVA

I was in my element.

I was where I belonged.

Completely alone in the silence, except for the gigantic bipedal tree creature with an affinity for spewing poison.

Home sweet home.

A glob of the foul stuff hissed as it ate away the earth beneath me. It was only inches from my boot, but I didn't flinch or try to move out of the way.

A rapid movement around a sorvuc was far more dangerous than its projectile poison. Its damn branches were covered in tiny neural fibers, capable of detecting incredibly small movements. The fibers were illuminated purple.

The sorvuc searched for me.

Under different circumstances, I would have found

it beautiful, but at that moment, it was just a pain in my ass.

The humidity made my short hair damp and scratchy. It clung to the curve of my neck. I longed to brush it away, but a movement like that would be a death sentence.

The luminescent purple faded away to a tranquil pink. I realized I was holding my breath.

Slowly, so slowly, I crept closer to the wide trunk of the sorvuc. I had already made an incision in its trunk. That's what pissed it off in the first place.

A necessary risk, but I only needed a few more drops of the thick scarlet fluid that seeped from the incision. The right person would pay a small fortune for its sap—or is it blood? Hell if I know.

As I slid my vial into place, ready to collect the liquid the sale of which would keep me comfortable for months, shouts erupted from somewhere nearby.

Damn it.

The sorvuc shrieked, its neural fibers flaring purple once again. It pivoted, razor-sharp leaves dangerously close to me. I rolled away, camouflaging my own movements in its rustling.

The hulking creature lumbered off in the direction the shouts came from—sort of. Its neural fibers must have picked up the sound vibrations, but with so many trees, it would have been difficult for the creature to determine the exact direction.

It's a good thing sorvuc had those fibers. They were as deaf as, well, a tree—at least, the sort of trees our ancestors brought over on their generation ship. But those trees sure as hell didn't fling poison or walk.

Walking plants were something the dense forest of Ankau had in excess. Even so, I'd take a hostile tree giant over people any day. At least they left me in peace.

Another round of shouts echoed through the trees. I clenched my teeth.

Speaking of peace.

I moved quickly and quietly through the dense forest, mindful not to disturb any of the thick vines that crisscrossed the forest floor. It was difficult to tell which ones were looking for a snack.

I spied a small herd of luurizi grazing between the roots of the docile Lenaus trees.

Their coats of lilac, sage, and pearl shimmered when they caught the mottled light bleeding through the canopy. Their silvery horns shone like jewels. It was easy to forget how deadly they were.

I was sure they could smell me.

Ordinarily, they would attack the moment they sensed an intruder. But this particular herd had become accustomed to my scent after so many years. It was an uneasy truce, but I still knew better than to take my eye off them.

Another bout of shouting brought me back to the present. It was louder this time. And stupider.

Clearly, whoever it was had a death wish, which was fine. I'd just prefer to be farther away when it happened.

The trees gave way to a small clearing. Two women, who I can only assume are the shouting morons, stood inches away from each other, their faces red with anger. They didn't notice my intrusion.

"You're not even trying anymore!" One woman, blonde and petite, hissed at the other. Her voice was tight, like she was trying to stay in control.

Sharp would have been the only way to describe her —sharp cheekbones, sharp chin, and sharp shoulders. Even her mouth was a sharp slash across her face.

I winced at her words, a headache throbbing at my temples. I almost wished something *would* come along and kill them.

"What more do you want me to do?" The other woman, dark-haired and softer than the other, answered wearily. "If I had known you were going to bring this up, I never would have agreed to meet you!"

Though they were different in coloring, they had the same nose and face shape. I guessed they were sisters—not that I cared.

"What other reason would there be to meet up?" the blonde snapped, her gray-green eyes narrowing. "What else do we have anymore?"

There was more poison in those words than there was in a fully grown sorvuc.

"I hate to interrupt," I said, startling both women.

I wanted to sound as annoyed as I felt, but my voice was brittle and raspy with disuse. I couldn't even remember the last time I had spoken aloud.

"But you really should shut up," I continued.

The blonde pivoted to face me. I was at least a head taller than her, but she somehow seemed bigger than she actually was. And the glare on her face would have made a narrisiri hesitate.

"This is none of your business," she said through clenched teeth.

"Nope, it isn't. I don't want to know about it. I don't care about it. But you really should find somewhere else to finish your screaming match," I replied.

"Do you think we're idiots? We have a howler with us," the blonde smugly fished a small black device from her pocket.

I hated those damn things. They emitted a high-pitched sound above the threshold of human hearing. It was meant to repel the creatures that stalked the forest, but I always thought it was a scam.

First of all, the people living in the cities and towns

hardly knew anything about the creatures that lived out here in the forest. Second, how would anyone know for a fact that a howler was working? No one could hear it.

"Yes, I do think you're idiots if you think that carrying a howler into the middle of aramirion territory during nesting season is a good idea," I snapped, fighting the urge to give the blonde a smug smile. "If they can hear that thing, you're screwed."

The dark-haired woman paled as she put her hand on the blonde's shoulder. The blonde stiffened at her touch.

"Leena, is that true?" the dark-haired woman whispered. Her eyes, the same color as the blonde's, nervously scanned the surrounding forest.

"How the hell would I know, Mariella? You're the one who moved all the way out to the middle of freaking nowhere!" the blonde, Leena, grumbled.

I turned to leave. Obviously, they had no intention of listening to me. Perhaps the dark-haired one, Mariella, might have seen reason, but Leena had some sort of chip on her shoulder—a chip the size of a damn ravine.

Fine. Whatever. They were adults.

I'd tried my best to warn them. It's not my fault if they chose not to listen to me.

What would I know, right? I've only been living out here for fifteen years. They would come to their senses and leave, or they would keep at it until one beast or another silenced them.

Either way, I got my forest and my silence back.

I could still feel their flurries of emotion as I marched through the undergrowth. If I was going to find another sorvuc to fill my vial, I needed to concentrate, but I couldn't do that with the feelings of two idiots in my head. I should turn back, try even harder to get them to leave.

A horrible screech unlike anything I had ever heard tore through the air. The sheer force of it drove me to my knees.

I tried to protect my ears with my hands, but it was useless. My vision blurred, stars danced behind my eyelids. I could practically feel my brain thrashing, desperate to escape that terrible sound.

Those idiots either did something to their howler, or the damn thing was malfunctioning. That had to be it.

As soon as I could get back on my feet, I staggered back to the clearing where I'd left the arguing pair. I would tear their stupid howler apart with my bare hands if I had to—anything to stop the noise.

"What the hell did you do?" I yelled.

Again, they didn't notice me when I entered the clearing, but, this time, they weren't distracted by an argument.

They stood side by side, looking up at the sky. Their faces were pale and their mouths were open in terror and confusion. I followed their gaze.

A jagged scar of pitch marred the once pristine stretch of endless blue.

The sky, *my* sky, had been torn open.

There was a beat of silence as if the whole planet had drawn in a collective breath of shock.

Then the forest erupted into chaos.

VREHX

Alarms blared around us. On the screen, all I could see were swirls of colors swallowing the Xathi.

The captain shouted orders to the rest of the crew, but his voice was distorted. It was changing—high-pitched then low and deep, fast then robotic, child-like then old, clear and loud, then soft and unintelligible.

Looking around the bridge, some of the colors were vibrant, glowing, and bright. Others were non-existent, as if all color had been drained, leaving behind various shades of gray.

Karzin's face twisted, melting down toward his midsection. I wanted to vomit, but Karzin's bird-like voice was chirping at me.

"TURN! IT! OFF!"

I turned my attention back to my control panel, just

to see it swirl around and fade. The screen was so bright, my eyes burned. The letters seemed to be dancing an old Skotan wedding march.

Looking up at the screen, the Xathi ship was ripped apart by the swirling vortex—no, it wasn't a vortex.

It was just a hole. Then it was a rip.

The only thing that stayed the same were the colors. Purple, white, and red streaks of color were covering the Xathi ship and reaching out for us.

The part of the Xathi ship already inside the rip was separating, coming apart at the seams. I could see part of the Xathi crew floating in space, then shredded by the force of the rip.

And we were getting closer to it.

I heard Rouhr's voice yelling out commands, for the engine room to go full speed ahead and drive the Xathi ship further into the rip.

It made sense. If the rip was doing this kind of damage to the "top" half, then it should destroy the rest of it as well. If we went with it, so be it.

The engines kicked in, and we were rocked forward as we crashed the *Vengeance* into the Xathi ziggurat. Our momentum pushed the Xathi ship further into the rip, and I watched as more and more of their vessels were ripped and disintegrated. It was only a few short breaths before the *Vengeance* herself began to fall through.

The energy inside her was incredible. The air carried a charge that made my scales tighten and my hair stand on end. Every color I had ever seen exploded in my eyes, bringing me a level of pain I had never felt before.

My mouth opened to scream, but no sound came out. It was as if my throat was burning and ripping in half vertically. I felt my skin and scales peel away from my body, exposing my muscles and bones to the emptiness of the void.

My eyelids, clamped as tight as I could hold them, broke apart and fell away, slowly exposing my eyes to the grayness of the void we had entered.

The bridge of the *Vengeance* was a bright gray, and everything else was varying shades of gray, getting darker and darker.

I looked at Rouhr to see his body falling apart like sand. He was yelling at us, but there was no sound.

That's when I realized that there was no sound at all. There wasn't a single solitary noise. Was the rip in space this quiet or had my ears been destroyed?

I moved my hand to touch my ear and stared in wonder at the stump at the end of my arm. I looked down, and my fingers were on my lap.

I wanted to retch. I wanted to die. I wanted to close my damn eyes.

I looked up at the screen to see the ziggurat, at least

the second half that we were attached to, reconstitute itself. It was rebuilding!

Then we were rebuilding, and the first of my senses to return was feeling. The pain was so much that I should have blacked out, except my eyelids weren't there.

When they finally returned, and I blinked for the first time, tears fell down my face. Finally, sound came back with an explosion of noise.

"...the hell is happening?"

"...are we?"

"Damage reports!"

"...off the damn switch."

"...switch, Vrehx!"

It felt as though forever was passing before my mind caught on to what they were wanting. I looked at my control panel and flipped the switch to the weapon. The void ended, and the alarms were back.

"Where the hell are we?" Rouhr asked.

"I'm not sure, Captain!" Sk'lar answered.

"Scan the—" Rouhr was interrupted as the ship shook violently, knocking most of us from our seats. "By all that is holy, what was that?"

Engineer Thribb's voice came on over the intercom. "We're losing engines, Captain. Partial power only. We've been caught by a gravitational field of some sort."

"What is generating the field?"

"I'm not sure, sir. My systems are inoperative."

"Sk'lar!"

"On it!" Sk'lar checked his system, letting out a curse that the translator didn't bother to translate. There was no need. "We're above a planet. Unfortunately, we are falling toward it."

He tried to keep his voice calm, but the slight vibrato betrayed his emotions.

The *Vengeance* wasn't built for the atmosphere of a planet. Our thrusters wouldn't work. If we fell into the atmosphere of a planet, we'd fall until we impacted with the ground, and it would be a very hard landing.

"Sir! The Xathi!" I called out, pointing at the screen.

The Xathi ziggurat was tilting, as if it were falling as well. Outside scanners adjusted and brought the full picture into view.

The planet was covered in green and blue, and above it, the Xathi ship tilted ever more as it fell.

"What planet is this, and where are the Xathi going to land?" Rouhr asked.

I brought up our positioning and the star maps in our database. "Sir, this is uncharted space for us. We don't have this planet or this system in our database."

Rouhr nodded, absorbing the information. "Crash site?"

Sk'lar turned to look at me, then at Rouhr. The look

on his face was silent resignation that something bad was going to happen.

"There appear to be seven main points of population on the planet. The Xathi are going to crash into the biggest concentration," Sk'lar said.

"Estimated survival?"

"Not good. Easily half of their city will be destroyed, killing thousands."

"And what of the Xathi? Will they survive the crash?"

"I'm not sure, sir. I'm not sure what the interior makeup of their vessel is, so I couldn't give you an accurate guess," Sk'lar replied, refusing to look at Rouhr as he stared at the computer.

"Engineer Thribb?"

"Captain?"

"Any chance of us breaking free and *not* crashing on the planet below?"

"Less than three percent, sir."

"Well, *groop.*" We all looked at Rouhr in shock. "Any way to get us away from civilization?"

"Easily, as long as our engines don't finish cutting out on the way down."

"Then keep us away from any population centers. The rest of you, brace for impact!"

We watched the Xathi ziggurat crash into the center

city, the largest city, as we strapped ourselves into our seats.

The cloud of dust and flame took out half of our sensors as we entered the atmosphere. We gained speed and tilted forward, and I could feel the pressure of the straps trying to hold me up as gravity pulled me downward.

It was a struggle to breathe. The pull of gravity was forcing us downward, while the atmosphere tried to resist our penetration. I tried to lift my arm to my console to push the button for the retro rockets in order to level us out and slow us down, but I couldn't lift my arm high enough.

The ground rushed at us, and I closed my eyes.

I'll be back with you soon, my family, I thought. My only hope was that we took those bastards with us.

My head snapped forward as the *Vengeance* crashed into the ground.

There was no way that death could possibly hurt this much.

I looked to my left to see Karzin slowly and gingerly lifting his head. Just past him, S'toz's head hung forward, his chin on his chest. To my right, Sk'lar was moaning in pain, trying to reach his arm up to his head.

I slowly—oh, so, so slowly reached up to unbuckle my straps. Now free from my restraints—and oh so grateful for them, as well—I gingerly got to my feet, waiting for the blast of pain to overwhelm my senses.

"Location?" I asked.

Sk'lar answered after a short coughing fit. "We're planet-side. That's all I know. Last thing I remember seeing was that we were heading for a large forest."

That's when it finally hit me. The computers were down.

"Captain?"

A groan from behind Sk'lar answered us. Rouhr's straps had snapped, and he ended up being flung around.

"I'm still alive. Vrehx?" He pulled himself to a sitting position on the floor, his right arm dangling, blood flowing from his cheek, and his left arm clutching his ribs.

"Sir?" My left arm hurt, and it was hard to breathe, I might have cracked a rib or six. I had a headache from the depths of destruction, and I was struggling to maintain weight on my right ankle.

"Get the commanders and your teams together. Find out where we are and if we're in danger. Thribb and I will handle the ship."

I knew better than to argue with him.

I made my way to the lift, but the doors wouldn't open.

I moved three steps to my left and opened the

maintenance hatch. Looking down, it was surprisingly clear.

Time to climb, I thought.

At least it was downward.

Click to get Vrehx now!

https://elinwynbooks.com/conquered-world-alien-romance/

NEED TO CATCH UP WITH THE STAR BREED?

Given: Star Breed Book One

When a renegade thief and a genetically enhanced mercenary collide, space gets a whole lot hotter!

Thief Kara Shimsi has learned three lessons well - keep her head down, her fingers light, and her tithes to the syndicate paid on time.

But now a failed heist has earned her a death sentence - a one-way ticket to the toxic Waste outside the dome. Her only chance is a deal with the syndicate's most ruthless enforcer, a wolfish mountain of genetically-modified muscle named Davien.

The thought makes her body tingle with dread-or is it heat?

Mercenary Davien has one focus: do whatever is necessary to get the credits to get off this backwater mining colony and back into space. The last thing he wants is a smart-mouthed thief - even if she does have the clue he needs to hunt down whoever attacked the floating lab he and his created brothers called home.

Caring is a liability. Desire is a commodity. And love could get you killed.

https://elinwynbooks.com/star-breed/

PLEASE DON'T FORGET TO LEAVE A REVIEW!

Readers rely on your opinions, and your review can help others decide on what books they read. Make sure your opinion is heard and leave a review where you purchased this book!

Don't miss a new release! You can sign up for release alerts at both Amazon and Bookbub:
bookbub.com/authors/elin-wyn
amazon.com/author/elinwyn

For a free short story, opportunities for advance review copies, release news and the occasional cat picture, please join the newsletter!
https://elinwynbooks.com/newsletter-signup/

And don't forget the Facebook group, where I post sneak peeks of chapters and covers!

https://www.facebook.com/groups/ElinWyn/

DON'T MISS THE STAR BREED!

Given: Star Breed Book One

When a renegade thief and a genetically enhanced mercenary collide, space gets a whole lot hotter!

Thief Kara Shimsi has learned three lessons well - keep her head down, her fingers light, and her tithes to the syndicate paid on time.

But now a failed heist has earned her a death sentence - a one-way ticket to the toxic Waste outside the dome. Her only chance is a deal with the syndicate's most ruthless enforcer, a wolfish mountain of genetically-modified muscle named Davien.

The thought makes her body tingle with dread-or is it heat?

Mercenary Davien has one focus: do whatever is necessary to get the credits to get off this backwater mining colony and back into space. The last thing he wants is a smart-mouthed thief - even if she does have the clue he needs to hunt down whoever attacked the floating lab he and his created brothers called home.

Caring is a liability. Desire is a commodity. And love could get you killed.

http://myBook.to/StarBreed1

Bonded: Star Breed Book Two

She doesn't need anyone. He's not going to let her go.

Eris Vance, salvager and loner, is happy with her life in the remote fringes of the Empire with just her AI for company. An abandoned ship could be the find of a lifetime, but it's not nearly as empty as she thinks. And the hulking man left behind kindles a heat she's never felt. But will he stay through the coming storm?

Connor is the perfect soldier - He's been made that way. Waking up to the destruction of the world he knew disturbs him almost as much as the gorgeous woman who found him. Her scent, her touch distracts him, and just this once, maybe he doesn't care.

The *Daedelus* is filled with secrets and the results of genetic experiments to breed the perfect soldier... and now that she's awakened him, the mystery of its destruction will hunt them both. Can the growing bond between them survive?

http://myBook.to/StarBreed2

Caged: Star Breed Book Three

No Past. No Trust. No Way Out.

Zayda Caiden relies on no one. An Imperial spy, her mission was betrayed - but she doesn't know the identity of the traitor.

And there's certainly no reason to trust the giant of a man dumped at the prison clinic, even if he makes her burn with feelings she thought long buried.

Mack has no memory, no real name. Just dreams of fire and pain, and a set of coordinates to a section of unexplored space he refuses to reveal. There's no room in his mission for a woman with secrets of her own, but her scent fills his dreams.

When they have a chance at freedom, can they trust each other enough to escape? Or will their secrets overwhelm their passion?

http://myBook.to/Starbreed3

Freed: Star Breed Book Four

When solitude leads to the brink of madness, only the touch of a sexy, headstrong doctor can pull a dangerous warrior back from the edge...

Dr. Nadira Tannu's work at the small clinic on Orem station was a quiet practice, helping the people of the Fringe. But then she and one of her patients were abducted into a nightmare on a long lost star ship and nothing would ever be the same.

When a rugged survivor rescues them, can she turn his thirst for revenge into a plan for escape? And can she keep her heart safe from the heat in his eyes?

Vengeance against the faceless droids who destroyed his brothers is all that keeps Ronan alive. But he can't resist the pleading look in a pair of wide green eyes staring at him from a cage.

He'll keep her safe. Even if it's from himself.

http://myBook.to/Starbreed4

Craved: Star Breed Book Five

Compassion. Kindness. Caring.

Not really part of my skill set. But for her, I might have to learn.

Geir

I run advance reconnaissance, collecting intel the Pack needs to execute our operations.

In and out, hard and fast.

And I don't need help.

So when a gorgeous woman saves my life, I'm knocked more than a bit off my game.

That's all it is.

Not the shy smile I hunger to coax from her lips, not the sweet body she keeps hidden. Not the mysteries that haunt her eyes.

And certainly not the bewitching scent that stirs me in ways no mission ever has.

I crave her like nothing I've found before.

Even if she might be the enemy, I'll make her mine.

Valrea

He can't save me.

The secrets of the Compound are too tangled. The nightmares in my blood can never be erased.

But his touch sends me reeling, thirsting for what I can't have.

What harm could one night do?

http://myBook.to/Starbreed5

Snared: Star Breed Book Six

When the only woman Xander cared for was ripped from his arms, nothing else mattered.

Now she's back. Fragile and brave, beautiful and brilliant. Someone to protect, someone to fight for.

Except she doesn't remember him at all.

Her curves and captivating scent drive him mad, demanding he cares for her, possess her.

He'll keep his mate safe, even if the Empire burns to ash around them.

Loree Sarratt is tired of everyone treating her like an invalid. Her hacking skills could save the Empire - if she's not arrested first.

First puzzle to solve? An overprotective pillar of muscle who turns her legs to jelly when he's in the same room.

She can't lose focus. But the heat of his gaze sends her pulse racing. His touch steals her breath. Everything tempts her to surrender...

And forget the danger she's in.

http://myBook.to/Starbreed6

ABOUT THE AUTHOR

I love old movies – *To Catch a Thief, Notorious, All About Eve* — and anything with Katherine Hepburn in it. Clever, elegant people doing clever, elegant things.

I'm a hopeless romantic.

And I love science fiction and the promise of space.

So it makes perfect sense to me to try to merge all of those loves into a new science fiction world, where dashing heroes and lovely ladies have adventures, get into trouble, and find their true love in the stars!

The Empire's Fringe – Science Fiction Romance

The Empire's Fringe Bundle

All of the below stories, at a special price!

https://elinwynbooks.com/the-empires-fringe/

Staked

In the slums of space station Cilurnum 8, fiercely independent Anisha Cheng must decide how far she's willing to trust Kieran Matthias, the one man who she's ever allowed to break her heart. If she can't, she risks losing the Sapphire Star, her late father's bar and the only home she knows, to a crime syndicate in three days. But as Anisha and Kieran try to work together, the plans of the syndicate may break them apart forever.

Jewel of Empire

On the spaceliner Dynomius, reformed cat burglar Audrey Pilgram has three weeks to prove her innocence of a series of copycat crimes, or all the sins of her past will be laid at her door. But her quest to uncover the culprit is complicated when she sees the next target - tall, handsome Phillip Lapsys. Can she stop the theft of the jewel before he steals her heart?

Raven's Heart

Jayna wasn't looking for trouble. Her plan was to keep her head down, save her money, and get back into to med school. But when she overhears the plans for a bio-terrorism attack that could wipe out the population of her station, her world is turned upside down. Raven's Heart is a steamy science fiction romance complete novella with a happy ending, containing nebula hot scenes of passion.

Stolen

An alien artifact. Archaeologist Eliya Cafeal has spent her life in pursuit of this find - and nothing is going to get in her way. Certainly not a rogue and a scoundrel, even if he makes her blood catch fire. Captain Ruvon Taxal likes his life. Few close friends, a spot of petty smuggling or charter trips as needed. No restrictions, and nothing to tie him down. And if his newest passenger, a feisty archaeologist with storm grey eyes, has gotten under his skin, well, he'll learn to live without her when she leaves. But everything is changed when Eliya is stolen.

Claimed

In the remote mountains of a frontier planet, tinkerer and part-time inventor Paige Roth has her hands full protecting her claim against the goons of

MagnorCo. With the help of her robots, she's doing pretty well, but the last thing she expects to fall into one of her traps is a handsome stranger trying to hike through the mountains for reasons of his own. He's handsome enough to make her forget where she put her toolkit, but can she trust him?

ALIEN WARRIOR ROMANCE

https://elinwynbooks.com/alien-romance/

Alien Mercenary's Desire: Alien Abduction Romance
Kordiss has spent his life on the fringe, not succumbing to his rages. But when he rescues feisty human Sharla from intergalactic sex traders, his defenses are breached by her trusting smile. And when she's stolen from his arms, nothing will stand in the way of getting her back.

This is a sexy, steamy stand-alone alien abduction short romance with a happy ending.